Mystery at School

New edition! Revised and abridged

By Laura Lee Hope

Illustrated by Pepe Gonzalez

Publishers · GROSSET & DUNLAP · New York

Look for these new
BOBBSEY TWINS® reissues:

Revised and abridged by Nancy S. Axelrad.

Contents

▪ 1 ▪
Trick Dog

"I suppose the Bobbsey twins have been solving mysteries all summer!" Danny Rugg said with a scornful laugh.

"As a matter of fact, we have," Bert replied coolly. He and his dark-haired sister, Nan, were twelve, the same age as their troublesome classmate.

Before Danny could speak again, Mr. Tetlow, their school principal, stepped toward the microphone on the stage of the auditorium.

"I am very pleased to tell all of you about our brand-new museum here at Lakeport Elementary School this year," he said. "We have some things already on display, but we will need more." His owlish eyes fixed on Bert. "That is why I've decided to form a special committee. Bert Bobbsey, will you please stand up?"

Six-year-old Freddie and Flossie, who were

seated in the front row, turned with the other first-graders and beamed at their brother.

"Bert," Mr. Tetlow continued, "you're in charge."

The boy cleared his throat nervously. "I am, sir?" he asked, hearing a snicker from behind.

"Tetlow's pet," Danny muttered under his breath while the principal explained that he hoped as many children as possible would help with the special museum project.

"Personally, I think it's a dumb idea," Danny said to his friend Jack Westley, whose nickname was Sneaker. "And besides, Bert Bobbsey's always made head of everything. It's really disgusting."

Sneaker agreed, causing Bert to flush angrily. Still, he had resolved that he would not let Danny annoy him this year, and so he said nothing as they made their way back to their classrooms.

When the final school bell rang, both sets of twins and their friends went immediately to the new museum room. It had been an empty classroom. Over the summer workers had painted it and had installed shelves and several glass cases.

"Ooh, look at this!" Flossie exclaimed, peering at a vase.

It had a large egg-shaped body and a narrow neck with a handle on each side. Small red horses pranced against a black background.

"I see you like my vase," Mr. Tetlow remarked from the doorway.

"It's bee-yoo-ti-ful!" Flossie said.

"It's called an amphora."

"Aaam-phaw-ruh?" Flossie's best friend, Susie Larker, repeated slowly.

"Yes. It was made in Greece several thousand years ago."

"I like the horses!" Freddie added. "They're chasing each other around and around."

Mr. Tetlow smiled. "The scene is a horse race," he said. "No doubt the amphora was given to the winner of one of the great athletic games."

"I like this statue best," Nan remarked, admiring a little female figure about eight inches tall. It had a regal-looking headdress of brilliant red and a dress of creamy-white and blue.

"Who is she?" asked Nellie Parks, a girl of Nan's age with silky blond hair and blue eyes.

"That is a statuette of the snake goddess," the principal replied. "She came from the ruins of an ancient palace in Crete. That's the largest of the Greek islands, in the eastern Mediterranean Sea."

As the other children gathered to look at the piece, Mr. Tetlow said, "She's the most valuable thing in our museum. A friend of mine, Mr.

Thomas Nelson, has loaned it to us while he is in Europe."

"We'll take extra special care of it, Mr. Tetlow," Bert promised.

"Good. I know Mr. Nelson is counting on that," the principal said, smiling. "So am I."

Although their visit was over, Bert and Charlie Mason lingered by a collection of Indian flints and arrowheads while Freddie and Teddy Blake stopped to look at the bows and arrows one more time. Finally they thanked Mr. Tetlow and started home. But talk about the new museum went on even after the group had separated at the corner.

"We'll have to get busy and find some more things to put on the shelves," Bert told his twin.

"The room *is* sort of empty, isn't it?" Nan said. "I know! We can ask everyone at school to bring in exhibits!"

"Yeah! That's a great idea! I just wish—" Bert stopped abruptly and looked around. "Did you hear that?"

"What?" Nan asked.

"That *pit-pat* sound. Someone is following us."

"I don't see anything," Freddie said, craning his neck.

"I do! I do!" Flossie exclaimed.

Again Bert shot around. "Where?" he asked, ready to swoop on the mysterious creature.

"There!" She giggled and pointed at a crest of shaggy white fur behind some shrubbery.

"It's a dog!" Bert laughed as the animal bounded forward, wagging his tail hello.

"Isn't he nice?" Nan said. "I wonder where he came from."

"Here, boy!" Bert snapped his fingers.

Instantly the dog hopped up on his hind legs and began to dance in a circle.

"What a funny doggy!" Flossie exclaimed.

At once he dropped on all fours again and ran over to the little girl, waving his fluffy tail.

"He's smiling at me!" Flossie exclaimed.

"Shake hands with him, Floss!" Freddie urged as the dog held out one paw.

When each of the children had shaken the dog's paw, Nan said, "He's very well trained, but don't play with him anymore. We don't want him to follow us home. His owner wouldn't like it."

"I wish he was ours!" Freddie said wistfully.

"Come on," his older sister said. "Let's go."

But as they turned down the next block, Bert observed the dog padding after them. "Go home!" he called out sternly.

The dog stopped, lay down, and put his head between his paws.

"He wants to come with us," Flossie said. "Maybe he doesn't belong to anyone!"

"She's right. He's probably just a stray," Bert put in. "He doesn't have a collar or a license."

"Even so, he can still have an owner," Nan countered, striding ahead of her brother.

"Don't you like doggies?" Flossie asked.

"Of course I do," Nan said, "but he doesn't belong to us." The dog barked as if he objected, and trotted after her. "Go home!" Nan said, and then she tried to ignore him. But the dog barked again.

By now the children had reached the sidewalk in front of their large rambling white house, and Dinah Johnson, the Bobbseys' housekeeper, hurried out. Upon seeing the furry creature, she narrowed her eyes and frowned.

"What's that?" she asked.

"A dog!" Flossie answered, giggling.

"I know it's a dog. But where did he come from?"

The small girl shrugged. "He followed us and he wants to live here."

"Live here!" The housekeeper gulped. "With Snoop? I don't think *he's* going to like that very much."

As she spoke, the black cat appeared in the doorway. Seeing the other animal, he hissed and arched his back, barring the entrance.

"See what I mean?" Dinah said.

6

"Come on, Snoop!" Bert pleaded. "The dog's not going to hurt you!"

The cat hissed again, arching his back higher.

Again Bert snapped his fingers, and the dog stood on his hind legs, prancing in a circle, while Snoop's eyes followed every move. Then the dog lay down in front of the cat, rolled over on his back, and held his paws helplessly in the air.

Freddie and Flossie cheered as Snoop's fur flattened out and he began to purr. The next moment he walked over to the dog and rubbed against his shoulder.

"They're going to be friends!" Freddie cried, running up and throwing his arms around both animals.

"Now all we have to do is persuade Mom and Dad to let us keep him," Bert said to Nan. "That is, if you don't mind."

"I don't mind if Snoop doesn't." She grinned.

At suppertime, after Mr. and Mrs. Bobbsey had met the shaggy new visitor, Dinah took the dog out to the kitchen. Soon he was eating side by side with Snoop.

"What shall we call him?" Flossie asked.

"How about Bongo?" Freddie suggested.

"Or Wrinkle Nose or Waggle Tail?" their father said teasingly.

The twins laughed.

"Why not call him Snap, because he does tricks when Bert snaps his fingers?" Nan said.

"What a good name!" said Bert. The other children agreed.

"Snoop and Snap?" said Dinah, shaking her head as she appeared in the doorway. "That's too much."

"I think it's cute," said Mrs. Bobbsey.

"Just remember," Mr. Bobbsey cautioned, "the dog isn't yours, and he probably has a name already."

"But, Daddy, we can keep him, can't we?" Freddie said in distress. He looked dolefully at his father. "Can't we, Daddy?"

Mr. Bobbsey shook his head. "That wouldn't be fair, son. The dog seems to be a valuable animal. His owner taught him a lot of tricks. We'll have to try to find him!"

Freddie sprang to his feet and ran over to his father, staring him right in the face. "You wouldn't make us give Snap back, would you?" he pleaded.

▪ 2 ▪

Snap Decision

"Freddie, dear," said Mrs. Bobbsey, "let's wait until morning to do anything further. We'll fix up a bed for Snap in the garage."

"Flossie and I can do it!" Freddie offered eagerly.

"Not tonight. You have school tomorrow. Dinah and I will do it," said Mrs. Bobbsey.

The children *were* tired after their first day back at school, and they went to bed early and fell asleep almost immediately.

Freddie and Flossie were up bright and early and ran out to the garage to see Snap.

"Snap!" Flossie cried, opening the door wide. The animal leapt toward them, then stood on his hind legs and marched a few steps.

"He likes it here!" Freddie said triumphantly.

During breakfast, the Bobbseys discussed ways of finding Snap's owner.

"We could put an ad in the paper," Bert suggested halfheartedly.

Nan ran to get some paper and a pencil, and the twins composed a notice for the "Found" column of the newspaper. It read:

> *FOUND: Trick dog. White, shaggy.*
> *Near Lakeport Elementary School.*
> *Owner please phone the Bobbseys at*
> — — — – — — — —.

"I'll call the ad in," Mrs. Bobbsey said. "You go on to school."

Just then Dinah called Bert to the phone. "It's Mrs. Mason," she told him.

Charlie's mother told Bert that her son had twisted his ankle the evening before. "I think he should stay off it today. He wants you to bring him the paper bag he left in his desk. Will you do that, please?"

"Of course, Mrs. Mason. I'll bring it at noon. I just hope it doesn't have yesterday's lunch in it." Bert chuckled.

But at noon Bert forgot about Charlie's message and went straight home. On the way back, however, he suddenly thought of it. "I'll get it now," he said to Nan. "There's still time to run over to the Masons'."

10

"Okay. I see Nellie anyhow. I want to talk to her."

While Bert ran into the school building, Nan walked toward her friend. She was standing with a group of children in front of a small green panel truck. Most of them were eating ice-cream cones, which they had bought at a newly opened shop down the street.

"Want a taste?" Nellie asked Nan, licking off some chocolate.

"No, thanks."

"Maybe she likes vanilla better," came a snickering voice from behind. Danny Rugg held out a half-eaten ice-cream cone.

Nan wrinkled her face disdainfully and stalked off. Bert was just coming out of the school with Charlie's package under his arm. He stopped to speak to the girls just as Freddie and Flossie, followed by Snap, ran toward them.

Gazing longingly at the rainbow of ice-cream cones, Freddie said, "I want one!"

"After school," Bert replied, catching sight of Snap, who was romping playfully among the children. "You shouldn't have brought *him* here!"

Flossie laughed. "He's smart enough!"

"He followed us," Freddie explained, "and we couldn't make him go back!"

11

"Oh, well, he'll probably leave when we go into the building. I hope so anyway," Bert said, starting off toward Charlie's house.

Just then a man in dirty coveralls came hurrying toward the truck. He was carrying a paper parcel, which he put in the back of the vehicle. Instantly Snap began to bark fiercely and ran forward.

The man, however, paid no attention and opened the door, ready to climb inside. Snap gave a flying leap, landing on the seat instead. Distracted by the noise, Bert turned around.

"Get out of here!" the driver snarled at Snap. He gave the dog a violent shove, which sent him sprawling to the ground. Then the man got in and started the engine.

"Snap!" Nan screamed. "Get out of the way!"

Like a streak of lightning, the dog scrambled to avoid being hit by the oncoming vehicle.

Bert, meantime, had pulled a small notebook out of his pocket and written down the license number.

"That man ought to be arrested!" the boy thought angrily, watching the truck race down the street.

"At least Snap wasn't hurt," Nan said. She leaned down to pet the whimpering animal. "Good boy, Snap. Good fella."

"Why did Snap bark at that man?" Flossie asked.

Bert shrugged. "I don't know. Maybe the man looks like someone Snap doesn't like!" he said. "See you later. I've got to run!"

Despite the interruption, the boy managed to get to and from Charlie's before the afternoon bell rang. He slipped into his classroom just as his teacher, Ms. Vandermeer, was about to close the door.

When school was finally over, Bert packed up his books and homework assignments and hurried to the museum room.

"Everyone's gone home. I guess I can lock up now," he decided.

Before turning out the lights, he glanced around. Everything appeared to be in order—until he noticed a strangely empty space on the shelf where the valuable statuette of the Cretan snake goddess had been!

"Oh, no!" Bert muttered in horror. "Who could have taken it?"

Frantic, he searched the room from one end to the other, but there was no sign of the little figure. Then he raced down the hall to the principal's office. Mr. Tetlow's secretary had left for the day, and the inner door was open.

"Excuse me, Mr. Tetlow," the boy said breathlessly.

The principal, who had been reading, looked up. "What's the matter, Bert?" he asked.

As quickly as he could, Bert blurted out the story of the missing statuette.

"But that's the most valuable thing we have in the museum!" Mr. Tetlow exclaimed. "We have to find it right away!"

His face grim and troubled, the principal bolted out of his office, followed by Bert. Despite Bert's previous search, they scanned each shelf in the museum room and opened all the cupboards. But the statuette was not there!

"We'll go through the whole building if we have to," Mr. Tetlow said. "I hope this isn't somebody's idea of a joke."

Bert couldn't help but think of Danny. He had said the museum was a dumb idea, and he was jealous of Bert for being given the honor of running it. But without proof, Bert knew he could not accuse the other boy.

After investigating every classroom and storage place and not finding the statue, Mr. Tetlow summoned the janitor. "Mr. Carter," the principal said, addressing the short chubby man, "were there any strangers in the building today?"

The man stared up at the basement ceiling as

15

he thought. "Yes, as a matter of fact, there were two. A man from some cleaning service. He said the district office sent him over."

"*Our* school district office?" Mr. Tetlow asked, obviously surprised.

"Yes, sir, Mr. Tetlow. They sent him over to see if he could help me with a couple of big jobs."

"But you said there were two people who came," Bert put in.

"The other man was from the electric company. He told me he had orders to check all the lights."

"What did he look like?" the principal inquired.

"I'd say pretty ordinary. Bald. And oh, he wore blue jeans. The cleaning-service guy was about my height and had real light-colored hair—almost white."

"Could one of them have taken the statuette?" Bert asked anxiously, looking at Mr. Carter.

"I guess so. But they both had ID's," the janitor said.

"Just the same, maybe we should call both companies," Bert said. "One of the ID's might have been fake."

"Good idea," said Mr. Tetlow. "If you're still as good at solving mysteries as you were, maybe you can solve this one!"

Mr. Carter gave Mr. Tetlow and Bert the number of the cleaning service, which they called right away. The manager confirmed the janitor's story, adding that his employee was extremely reliable.

Mr. Tetlow thanked him for the information. Then he phoned the electric company. When he asked about the man who had come to check the lights, the official sounded surprised. "I don't know what you're talking about. We didn't send anyone to your school today."

Mr. Tetlow persisted and gave as complete a description of the visitor as he could.

"All our men wear shirts with the company name on it," said the voice on the phone. "It's against regulations not to."

Mr. Tetlow put down the phone and frowned. "It must have been the guy who told Carter he was from the electric company!" the principal said gloomily.

"Let's notify the police at once," Bert said, and Mr. Tetlow nodded.

When he was finished talking to the police department, he advised Bert to stay awhile. "Chief Mahoney is sending someone over to talk to us."

Within a few minutes a police car stopped in front of the school, and an officer darted into the building.

"Just where was the statue when it was stolen?" Officer Jim Murphy asked briskly.

Mr. Tetlow and Bert led the way to the museum and showed him the shelf where the snake goddess had stood on display. Officer Murphy gazed intently at the now-empty space.

"It's impossible to tell anything from fingerprints. There are too many of them," he said, strangely puzzled. "You say this is the only thing missing?"

Bert nodded.

"It also happens to be worth the most money," Mr. Tetlow revealed. "Whoever stole the statue must've known its value."

As the questioning continued, Bert told about the mysterious man who had told the janitor he had come to check the lights. "The electric company says it didn't send anyone," Bert added.

After getting a full description from Mr. Carter, Officer Murphy closed his little notebook. "I hope we can pick him up soon."

While all of this was happening, Freddie and Flossie were at home with Nan. Curled up comfortably on the living-room couch, Nan was reading a mystery story and did not hear the younger children go outside with Snap.

Flossie picked up a long stick, at which Snap

made little whining sounds. "I think he wants to jump over it," she said.

"Try him," Freddie urged.

Flossie held the stick straight out about two feet off the ground. "Come on, Snappy," she said as the animal backed away. With his tongue hanging out, he bolted forward with a high leap. "Snap knows another trick!" the little girl exclaimed.

"I wonder if he'll jump over the water from the hose," Freddie said, attaching it to the outlet. "I'll squirt it over there. You stand on the other side and call Snap. Okay?"

Flossie obeyed gleefully, but the dog refused to jump. Instead, he hopped about, barking sharply.

"Come on, Snappy!" Flossie encouraged him. "You won't get wet if you jump high enough!"

Freddie lowered the stream and his sister called again. This time the dog cleared the water perfectly. Then he turned around and leapt back again.

"See! He likes it!" Flossie cried excitedly.

Snap jumped back and forth until he was dripping wet. Just then Dinah poked her head through the front door. "Hey, what's going on out here?" she called.

As Flossie ran toward her, the dog trotted behind. When he had finally caught up, he shook himself vigorously and sneezed.

"Stop!" Flossie exclaimed. "You're getting me all wet!"

Without thinking, Freddie, who was still holding the water hose, swung it in Flossie's direction. Flossie jumped aside but slid on the slippery grass.

"Flossie! You come in here this minute and put on some dry clothes!" Dinah commanded, casting a serious glance at Freddie. "And you put that hose away, you hear me?"

"Oh, all right," Freddie said meekly.

He had just started dragging the long green tube across the lawn when Danny Rugg passed by. "Hi, Freddie!" he said cheerfully.

Freddie, who did not trust Danny, murmured a greeting and went on with his work.

"Sneaker just told me something was stolen from the museum! He was at school when it happened," Danny volunteered.

Freddie said nothing.

"And I know who stole it, too!" the other boy went on, preening like a peacock.

"Who?" Freddie asked curiously.

"Your brother, Bert!"

■ 3 ■

Ping-Pong Puppets

"My brother never stole anything!" Freddie declared hotly.

"Oh, no?" Danny smirked. "Well, I saw him with my very own eyes. He was coming out of school after lunch with a package under his arm. And it *wasn't* his lunch!"

"He was taking something to Charlie Mason!" Freddie's voice rose to a shout.

"Sure, sure," Danny jeered.

By this time Freddie was so furious he could hardly speak. He wanted to punch Danny, but he knew he was too little to hurt him.

"You get out of here!" Freddie cried, blasting the hose in the other boy's direction.

Caught by surprise, Danny froze in the misty spray. Then, with a yell, he ran to the end of the sidewalk.

Water dripping from his face, Danny shook his fist at Freddie. "I'll get even with you, Fred-

die Bobbsey!" he spouted as he dashed away.

Snap, who had been watching the two boys, raced after Danny, barking ferociously.

"Come back, Snap!" Freddie called, stopping the dog in his tracks.

Hearing the commotion, Nan put down her book and went to the window. Bert, with a glum expression on his face, was just coming up the front steps with Freddie and Snap.

"What happened?" she asked, opening the door quickly.

Bert explained about the disappearance of the ancient statuette. "It's all my fault," he said gloomily. "I'm supposed to be in charge of the museum!"

"That was my favorite exhibit, too!" Nan lamented. "But it's not your fault if somebody took it."

Freddie spoke up. "Danny came by before. He says you did it, Bert."

Overhearing the remark from the stairway, Flossie said, "Bert never stole anything! Never ever!"

"That's what I told Danny!" her twin explained. "I turned the hose on Danny and he ran!"

"You did?" Flossie said in awe. Then she laughed.

"I hope he doesn't start spreading the story

around school. He's mean enough," Nan said to Bert.

"Well, what am I supposed to do?" Bert grumbled.

"I told Danny you were taking something over to Charlie," Freddie said.

But Bert knew how little the truth mattered to Danny. He would twist it any way he could to make trouble for the twins.

"I wonder who did take the snake goddess," Nan put in.

"For a split second I thought maybe it was Danny," Bert admitted. "Mr. Tetlow and I looked all over the building before we called the police. Now we think it was a guy pretending to be from the electric company."

Although nothing more was said about the missing statuette that evening or at school the next morning, Bert had not forgotten Danny's accusation.

At noon, as he was leaving school, he challenged Danny. "So, you think I stole the statue!" Bert said angrily.

"Yes, I do, and I'm going to tell the police everything!" the bully declared. "That peanut brother of yours can't turn the hose on me and get away with it!"

"Apologize!" Bert persisted.

"Me, apologize?"

"Yes, you!"

By this time the boys had reached the playground. Danny gave Bert a shove that sent him staggering against the side of the building.

Although smaller than Danny, Bert was strong. He regained his balance quickly and advanced on the other boy with clenched fists, causing Danny to punch back as hard as he could.

Suddenly Mr. Tetlow saw the boys and shouted, "Hey, you two, quit it!" Bert and Danny turned quickly as the principal strode forward.

"He started it!" Danny complained.

Mr. Tetlow folded his arms and looked at Bert. "Go ahead," he said. "I'm waiting for an explanation."

"He told my brother I stole the statue," Bert replied.

"Danny, I'm ashamed of you," Mr. Tetlow said. "You know that isn't true."

The freckle-faced bully dug his heel into the dirt. "Yes, sir," he replied.

"Now, apologize to Bert and go on home to lunch!"

Gritting his teeth, Danny mumbled something and hurried away.

Mr. Tetlow put his hand on Bert's shoulder. "Don't worry about the statuette," he said kindly. "I'm sure the police will find it."

"I hope so, Mr. Tetlow."

But at the end of the afternoon Bert was gloomier than ever. Nan called to him and Charlie as they were leaving their classroom.

She had discussed the situation with Nellie, and between them they had decided to try cheering the downhearted boy.

"Nell and I got some stuff to make puppets out of," Nan said. "We thought maybe we could have a show and raise money for the museum."

Bert smiled bleakly.

"Do you want to help us?"

"Sure," Charlie said, pulling his friend along. "Come on, sourpuss."

In a little while the four children were settled around the Bobbseys' dining-room table. Paste, crayons, and bits of material were strewn everywhere.

"What are the Ping-Pong balls for?" Charlie asked, letting one skitter across the table.

"They're for the heads," Nellie explained. "The man at the store made a hole in each one just big enough for a finger to fit inside. All we have to do is draw faces on the balls and make costumes.

"I guess we could've bought hand puppets,"

26

Nan said, "but we thought this would be more fun."

Charlie said he wanted to make a policeman, while Nan and Nellie decided on animals—an ostrich and a sweet little kitten.

"What about you, Bert?" his sister asked. "What are you going to make?"

Bert, who had been staring out the window, didn't answer.

"How about a clown?" Nellie said. "A happy one with a great big smile!"

"Okay." Bert sighed. As it turned out, his was the easiest to do. He drew a wide red mouth on the Ping-Pong ball, a round black nose, and two big gaping eyes. Then he folded a piece of red paper into the shape of a cone and pasted it onto the head.

"I'll make the suit if you'll fix the ostrich head," Nan offered.

For the first time since they had gotten home, Bert smiled. He set to work covering the ball with gray crayon and drew large eyes with long lashes on them. Then he made a wide bill from a piece of brown paper and pasted it on.

"This will be the long neck," he said, holding up a tube of cardboard. He fastened one end to the hole in the Ping-Pong ball.

In a little while Nan had finished the clown suit. It was made of red-and-white-dotted material, and at the ends of the sleeves she had attached tiny red-cloth hands stuffed with cotton.

Bert pasted the suit to the head. Then he stuck his index finger into the hole at the back and put his middle finger and thumb into the two arms.

"Ho, ho!" he laughed, making the clown's hands beat against its chest while the head tossed back and forth.

"That's fantastic, Bert!" Charlie said admiringly. "But wait until I finish my policeman! Your clown won't have much to laugh about!"

Charlie had colored his Ping-Pong ball tan and began drawing a very serious face on it, including a red line for the mouth, over which he pasted a paper mustache.

"The only thing missing is his cap," the boy said, cutting some blue paper.

When the puppet was finished, Nellie cried, "He's terrific! Can you make a kitten's head for me, too?"

While Charlie did this, the girls sewed the bodies for the other three puppets.

Then Nellie looked at the clock. "Oh!" she exclaimed. "It's getting late. I'd better go home."

"I guess I should, too," Charlie said, helping Nan and Bert put everything away.

Afterward, Nan mentioned the ad about Snap

they had put in the newspaper. "I wonder why no one has answered it yet."

"Maybe Flossie was right. Maybe he doesn't belong to anyone and we can keep him!" Bert observed, putting the top on the paste jar.

All this time the younger twins had been at Susie Larker's house playing. Now they came running up the front steps. As Freddie turned the doorknob, Flossie leaned over to pick up something on the landing.

"It's a letter! It must have dropped out of the mailbox!" she said, stepping inside with Freddie. "Nan? Bert? Here's a letter, and it says it's for the Bobbsey twins!"

"We're in the dining room!" Nan called back. In the next moment she was opening the envelope and pulling out a piece of lined paper.

"It's from a man who says he thinks we have his trick dog!"

"Really?" Bert said.

"Where does he live?" Freddie asked while Flossie sniffled back tears.

Nan studied the letter again, then turned the envelope over in her hand.

"That's funny," she said. "He doesn't give any address or telephone number."

"What's his name?" Bert said anxiously.

"James Smith."

"Maybe we can find him in the phone book."

Bert went to the hall table to get it. He flipped the pages until he came to the Smiths and ran his finger down the column.

"There are three James Smiths and two J. Smiths," he announced. "I suppose we'll have to call all of them."

"I want to call first!" Flossie declared.

"Okay," said Nan. Flossie ran to the hall phone and pressed the numbers as Bert gave them.

There was a long wait, then a little voice said, "Hello."

"Is this James Smith?" Flossie asked. "And did you lose a dog?"

"I'm Sally Smith," the voice answered indignantly. "I don't have a dog."

"Sally!" Flossie exclaimed. "This is Flossie!"

The girls were in the same room at school. "Are you sure your daddy didn't write us a letter?"

"I don't think so," came the uncertain answer, "but I'll ask him when he comes home."

"You have the wrong Smith, Flossie," Nan whispered. "Say good-bye and hang up!"

Freddie made the next call. This time the person who answered had a thin, quavery voice. "What's that?" the old man asked.

The little boy repeated the question. "Haven't

had a dog for fifty, sixty years! But if you want to get rid of yours, I'd be glad to take him!" he cackled.

"Oh, no! We want to *keep* him!" The little boy dropped the receiver as if it had turned red-hot.

After Bert and Nan had made the last three calls, Nan said, "You know what? I have a hunch that letter wasn't written by any James Smith! And I think I know who did write it!"

▪ 4 ▪
Twin Traps

"What makes you think James Smith didn't write the letter?" Bert asked Nan.

"I just remembered that we never put our address in the ad," said Nan.

"Mr. Smith could have looked up our address in the phone book," Bert replied.

"If he went to all that bother, why wouldn't he just have phoned?"

For once, Bert had no answer.

"Besides," Nan continued, "the writing doesn't look like a grown-up's. Also, if the person really thought Snap was his dog, why didn't he give us his address?"

Bert took the letter and examined it carefully. "You're right," he said.

"I think our letter writer is none other than Danny Rugg!" said Nan.

"Then we can still keep Snap!" Flossie cried.

"Yes, but first we have to prove the letter is a

hoax," her brother mused. He thought for a minute. "I've got it!" He told the others his plan.

The next morning on the way to school Bert told Nellie and Charlie what he was going to do. Then before the bell rang he had a conversation with Ms. Vandermeer.

As soon as the children were all assembled, she told them that Bert had an announcement to make.

He rose from his desk and walked past Danny, who was slouched in his chair as usual. "Teacher's pet," Danny whispered nastily, watching Bert saunter to the front of the room.

Bert's eyes traveled past Danny's as he spoke. "You know Mr. Tetlow is hoping that all of us can bring something to exhibit in the museum," Bert told the children. "Nellie, Charlie, and I would like to know what you have. So will you write down anything you can contribute?"

When everyone had finished, Charlie collected the papers and gave them to Bert.

"Thanks," he said. "The committee will let you know what we can use."

At recess time Bert and Nan joined their friends in a corner of the room, where they had already started to sort through the mountain of paper. There were all kinds of suggestions.

"Hey, here's one for a rattlesnake skin!" Charlie exclaimed.

"And somebody else has an old embroidered shawl from Spain!" Nellie said.

"Where is Danny's paper?" Nan asked.

"Here it is!" The other girl held up a piece of lined notebook paper. "I've got a big fat NOTHING for your dumb museum" was scrawled across it in giant letters.

Nan took the paper while Bert pulled the mysterious letter from his pocket. They laid them on a desk side by side. The paper and the writing matched perfectly!

"So it *was* Danny!" Nan said, narrowing her eyes.

"What are you going to do?" her girlfriend asked.

Before either twin could answer, however, the bell signaling the end of the recess period rang. The other children came in and took their seats. Danny, the last to arrive, seemed strangely flustered.

"Something's happened! Look at him!" Nan whispered to Bert, who glanced at his troublesome classmate with mild curiosity.

During recess Freddie and Flossie had met the bully in the hall.

"Hi! How's the little hose squirt?" Danny said to Freddie.

34

The little boy did not answer.

"Can't talk, huh? Do you want to see another good trick?"

"What is it?" Freddie asked uncertainly.

Danny led the small twins to a drinking fountain that stood against the wall of the corridor.

"See this?" he asked, pointing to the water-spout.

Freddie nodded.

"Well, you step on the pedal to start the water," Danny explained, "while you put your finger over the hole."

Freddie looked doubtful.

"Go on! Do it and see what happens!"

Still somewhat hesitant, Freddie put his finger over the spout and stepped on the pedal. The water spurted in all directions!

Mr. Tetlow had just come out of his office and started down the hall when a long stream of cold water caught him right in the eye! Danny fled down the hall and disappeared into the classroom.

"Freddie Bobbsey!" the principal said sternly. "Follow me!"

With Flossie at his side, the small boy walked slowly into the principal's office. Angry, Mr. Tetlow sat down behind his desk.

"Don't you know that it is against the rules of

this school to play with the water fountain?"

Freddie hung his head. "Y-y-yes," he confessed.

Flossie spoke up. "It wasn't his fault, Mr. Tetlow. Danny Rugg said he'd show him a good trick. Freddie didn't know what it was."

Mr. Tetlow sighed. "Danny Rugg again! Well, you stay away from him," he warned. "But if I ever see you playing with that drinking fountain again, you will be punished!"

Freddie gulped. "Yes, sir," he said. "I won't do it again."

"All right. You and Flossie go back to your room. I'll see Danny Rugg later."

That afternoon Bert met the principal in the hall. "Have you heard anything about the statue?" the boy inquired.

"Not a word."

"May I call the police? Maybe they've found something and just haven't told us yet."

Mr. Tetlow stroked his chin thoughtfully. "Do it now, why don't you?"

Accepting the suggestion, Bert put in the call and was shortly connected with Chief Mahoney. He asked if there had been any progress in the search for the missing statue.

"None so far," the officer said. "But we did have a report from the police in Sanderville. There has been a whole string of thefts at the museum over there. Each one was different, and museum security wasn't able to do a thing about them."

"Do you think they're connected with ours?" Bert asked.

"Let's say that in every case, only the most valuable exhibits were stolen," the chief said. "The thief seems to know something about fine art."

Bert thanked the chief for the information and hung up. When he told Mr. Tetlow the details, the principal sat back in his chair. "I hope they catch the thief before Mr. Nelson comes back from Europe. I don't want to have to tell him his snake goddess is gone!" he said.

When classes were over, Bert and Nan met their friends in a specially assigned room to work on the puppet show. Bert and Nan had brought the puppets to school for a rehearsal. They didn't know that Freddie and Flossie were hanging around outside.

"Bert's really upset about that statue!" Flossie said sadly.

"Maybe we can help him! We know how to look for clues!" Freddie exclaimed.

Hopeful, the two children went back into the school and down the hall to the museum room.

"We need a magnifying glass!" Freddie said.

"Daddy has one!" Flossie replied.

"But we need it now!"

The pair walked slowly around the room, examining the shelves and the floor as well.

"Here's something!" Freddie said. He stooped to pick up a chewing-gum wrapper that lay behind the door. "I'll bet the thief dropped it!"

"Oh, Freddie! Anyone could have dropped that!"

"But we're not allowed to have gum in school," the boy pointed out. "And anyway, I never saw any of our friends chewing this kind. Let's see if we can find something else."

The twins explored all the classrooms and the auditorium, too. They found schoolbooks, notebooks, pencils, combs—all sorts of misplaced articles—but nothing else.

"We should look outside under the museum window," Freddie suggested finally. "The thief might have left footprints."

Outside the building Freddie and Flossie hurried around to the side. To their dismay they found no footprints, and the plantings appeared undisturbed.

"I guess he didn't go in through the window," Flossie remarked.

Disappointed, they started toward the rear door. Then suddenly, just as they reached it, Flossie noticed something in the shrubbery. She reached into the prickly bushes and pulled out an odd-looking item.

▪ 5 ▪
A Bald Clue

"What's this?" Flossie asked in bewilderment. She held up a piece of flesh-colored rubber with a fringe of human hair around the edge.

"Yuck!" the little girl cried, dangling the strange find at arm's length.

Freddie took it from her. "Maybe you've found a clue!" he said excitedly. "Let's show it to Bert."

At once the children hurried back into the school building.

When they came to the room where their brother and sister were rehearsing, Freddie burst out, "Look what Flossie found!"

Nan put down the ostrich puppet as her little brother explained that he and Flossie had been hunting for clues to the thief of the snake goddess. "And Flossie saw this in the shrubbery by the back door!" he ended, waving it in the air.

Bert asked to see it. "I think it's part of a wig," he said.

"But it has so little hair," Nan objected as the younger children gathered close to Bert.

"It's a bald wig!" he explained. "You know, the kind someone would wear to look bald."

"Bert!" Nan gasped suddenly. "Didn't Mr. Carter say that the phony electrician was bald?"

Her brother's eyes glistened. "Yes!"

"So if the man wasn't really bald," Nan continued, "he could even have been that truck driver—the one who tried to run down Snap!"

"The truck driver!" Nellie exclaimed.

"He was here the same day the statue was taken! And when he came back to the truck, I remember he was carrying a package!"

"I'm going to call Chief Mahoney from the principal's office right now and tell him!"

"Well, it's a help knowing we're not looking for a bald man," said the chief when he heard about Flossie's discovery. "Your hunch about the connection between him and the truck driver sounds good to me. But what *did* the man look like?"

Bert tried to remember. "Light-brown hair, I think. Average height, average build. I mostly remember his dirty coveralls and all the commotion Snap caused."

The chief thanked Bert and said, "I'll send

Officer Murphy out to get the piece of wig for evidence."

The children were too excited to continue the puppet rehearsal. They talked to Mr. Tetlow a few minutes, then went outside and sat on the front steps to wait for the policeman.

When Officer Murphy arrived, Bert explained how Flossie had discovered the clue behind the school building. "It's just a hunch, but we think the thief was a truck driver who parked over there." He pointed toward the curb next to the driveway.

"When no one was watching," Bert continued, "he put on a bald wig to disguise himself and told the school janitor he was sent to check the lights. What we can't figure out, though, is why he was wearing different clothes. Mr. Carter said he was wearing jeans, but we saw him in coveralls."

"He probably took off the jeans and his shirt to be sure no one recognized him when he left. After all, he was parked in plain view of the school."

"I've been wondering about that, too," Nan said. "Why would a thief park right in front like that?"

"Well, most likely, he was working alone and wanted to get away as fast as possible."

"But it was just after lunch and a whole bunch of us saw him leave. We can identify him."

"Maybe. Do you think any of the other kids got a good look?" the officer asked. "Chances are he had planned to escape before you all came back for the afternoon session and maybe he was delayed. In any case, he didn't seem too concerned about it."

Bert flashed a grin. "I wrote down the license number of his truck!" he clucked, putting his hand in one pocket, then another. "I don't have my notebook with me. It must be at home. I'll get the number and call you."

"Fine. I'll take this new evidence to headquarters right away!" Officer Murphy replied, congratulating the children. "Keep up the good work!"

Eager to look for his notebook, Bert said good-bye to Nellie and Charlie and rushed home with his brother and sisters. The moment they arrived, he began to hunt for the notebook. Unable to find it, he went to see if Dinah was around. She was in the basement, dusting and vacuuming the closet where the family stored their summer clothes.

"Did anyone phone about the ad for Snap?" Bert asked.

Sneezing into a tissue, Dinah pulled herself

out of the closet and looked up. "What did you say?"

The boy detective repeated the question.

"The phone hasn't rung all day."

"Also, have you seen that little brown notebook I had? I can't find it anywhere."

"Did you check the kitchen?" Dinah said, sneezing again. "Excuse me."

Bert nodded. "God bless you."

"How about the shelf in the garage? Maybe you left it there when you cleaned the car yesterday."

"Thanks!" Bert hurried out the back door. But in a few minutes he returned with a worried look. "It isn't there," he reported. "And I think I did leave it on that shelf!"

"It has to be someplace," Nan insisted. "Come on. I'll help you look for it."

They searched thoroughly, but with no success. "Officer Murphy won't think I'm such a good detective now!" the boy concluded miserably.

"He will, too," Nan consoled her twin. "I'm sure it'll turn up!"

Mr. and Mrs. Bobbsey were interested to hear about the wig clue when Nan told them about it at supper. "I think you children are doing a very good job!" their mother said proudly.

At that moment Snap nudged open the door from the kitchen.

"What's that in his mouth?" Mr. Bobbsey asked.

"Here, boy!" Bert called.

Obediently Snap trotted toward him and laid something on Bert's knee.

It was the missing notebook!

"Snap found your notebook!" Flossie exclaimed.

Her brother picked up the little brown book and leaned down to pat the dog. "I wonder where it was," Bert said, letting Snap nuzzle his leg. "If only you could talk."

"He sleeps in the garage. Maybe he took it off the shelf where you left it!" Nan proposed.

"Ask him!" Freddie urged.

"Snap's smart, but he's not that smart!" Bert said.

After supper he telephoned police headquarters. Officer Murphy had gone off duty, but the boy left the license number of the truck with the policeman in charge.

"We'll track it down as fast as we can," the officer promised. "Thanks."

The next afternoon Nan and Bert met Nellie and Charlie to finish rehearsing for the puppet show. When they were done, Nellie mentioned

Danny Rugg. 'We still haven't figured out how to pay him back for sending you that awful note about Snap!" she said.

"He's always making fun of us solving mysteries," Nan commented.

"I know!" Bert broke in. "Let's make him think he can find the missing statue!"

"How?" Nellie asked. "Even we don't know where it is."

Bert thought hard. "Why not write Danny a note telling him he can find the statue at some deserted place?"

Everyone agreed on the plan, and Nellie printed a message that said:

> *If you want to show you're a better detective than the Bobbseys, you can find the missing snake goddess at Jimmy's Pizza Plaza on Route 16.*
>
> *A friend*

Nan laughed. "Perfect! Can't you just see Danny's face when he gets this?"

Charlie and Nellie agreed to mail the note on their way home. "He'll have it tomorrow afternoon!" Charlie said, chortling to himself.

That evening, however, as Bert settled down to do his homework, the telephone rang. It was Chief Mahoney.

"We've checked that license number, Bert," he reported, and explained that the license had been issued to a car-rental agency. Upon checking with the company, he learned that the truck had been rented to a man named Ernie Perry.

"Ernie Perry? Who's he?" Bert asked.

"He works at the home of a Mr. Nelson."

The boy's lips parted in astonishment. "Mr. Nelson owns the statuette! Perry couldn't be the thief!"

"It does seem strange, I know," Chief Mahoney admitted. "We're going to send a detective over to Nelson's house to talk to Perry. I'll let you know what we find out."

Bert thanked the chief, then went to tell Nan and the other twins the news. They all agreed it was a very odd situation indeed.

"But if Perry works for Mr. Nelson, why would he go to all the trouble of stealing the statuette from the school? He could've taken it from the house when he had the chance," Nan said.

"Maybe he was planning to steal it after his boss went away," Bert replied.

"You mean he didn't count on Mr. Nelson loaning it to the school?"

"Exactly. But then he realized he had the perfect cover-up," the boy went on. "No one would

47

suspect Mr. Nelson's employee of taking the statuette from the school."

"Least of all Mr. Nelson," Nan concluded.

During recess the next day the boy told Mr. Tetlow what the police had learned about the truck driver.

"Do you know what Ernie Perry looks like, sir?" Bert inquired.

"I've never met the man," Mr. Tetlow replied, adding that Mr. Nelson had always spoken well of Perry. "Apparently he has been a great help to Mr. Nelson. An all-around caretaker, you might say, with an interest in art."

"Has he been there a long time?" Bert asked.

"With Mr. Nelson? Oh, maybe six months. He started right after the previous man retired to Arizona."

"Chief Mahoney is going to send an officer to investigate. Maybe that will solve the mystery."

But when Bert went home a little while later, he received disappointing news from the police chief. "Our men couldn't locate Perry this morning. There was no one at the Nelson house."

After reporting this to the other children, Bert said, "It looks as if the disappearance of the statuette is as much of a mystery as it ever was!"

▪ 6 ▪

Circus Star

Nan gave a mischievous laugh. "Don't forget Danny is going to find it for you!"

"I wonder if he got the letter," Bert replied. "Charlie and I are ready to follow him on our bicycles if he takes off after school!"

All afternoon Danny seemed to be in a triumphant mood. He even volunteered to help Ms. Vandermeer when she had difficulty opening a window.

"Thank you, Danny," she said, pleased by his change of attitude.

"Oh, you're welcome," the boy answered modestly.

"He is such a phony," Bert told his sister at the end of the day.

As they stood outside the building waiting for Danny to appear, he strolled right up to them. "I thought you were such great detectives!" he said. "You can't even find an old statue that was stolen out from under your noses!"

Bert winked at Nan. "Maybe you can do better!"

"I know I can!" Danny exclaimed cheerfully, and sauntered off.

Bert caught Charlie's eye as they watched Danny go over to the bicycle rack. He pulled his bike out, hopped on, and rode down the driveway. When he had turned the corner, Bert and Charlie ran to get *their* bicycles.

"Good luck!" Nan called after them.

"He's going to Route Sixteen!" Charlie observed as the boys spotted Danny ahead of them.

"I'd love to be there when he rides up!" Bert snickered.

"We can take a shortcut by going up Elm Street!"

"You're on!" Bert said, and they began to pedal faster.

The two boys rode in silence until they were out of town. Then, as they veered onto a road that brought them to Route 16, the young detective remarked, "I'm sure we've beaten him!"

Charlie looked back along the highway. There was no sign of Danny. "If he doesn't show up, the joke's on us!"

"When he talked to Nan and me, he sounded

as if he knew just where to find the snake goddess!"

Jimmy's Pizza Plaza was a low clapboard building with counters all around the outside. The kitchen, in the middle, had wooden blinds drawn over it, and fastened to them was a large sign that said:

CLOSED FOR THE WINTER
OPEN MAY 15

Bert and Charlie rode up to the deserted restaurant. "Let's hide behind one of these front counters," Bert suggested. "We can watch him when he comes."

"He'll see our bikes," Charlie objected.

"No he won't. We can put them behind that little building over there!" Bert pointed to a nearby shack.

The two boys quickly slid off their seats and stood the bicycles against the far wall of the dilapidated structure.

"Hurry!" Charlie cried. "I see him!"

They had just climbed over the front counter and hidden themselves when Danny arrived on his bicycle. He dismounted and peered around uneasily. Then, trying to appear confident, he leaned against the counter and stared out at the road.

It was all Bert and Charlie could do to keep from laughing out loud! After a few minutes Danny began to pace up and down. Then he strolled around the outside of the building.

But as he returned to the front again, an old car drove up and a rough-looking man got out. He walked toward the restaurant. For a moment Danny acted uncertain, but raised his courage long enough to say hello.

"Do you know where the snake goddess is?" he asked somewhat shakily.

Stopping abruptly, the stranger glared at Danny from head to toe. "What are you talking about, kid?" he asked hoarsely. "I don't know anything about snakes or goddesses. I just want to get a pizza."

"S-sorry!" Danny stammered. "The r-restaurant's closed!"

Giving the boy a disgusted look, the stranger stepped back into his car and left. Bert and Charlie whooped with laughter!

"Who's there?" Danny shot back, staring at the counter. The two boys stood up.

"Are you James Smith, by any chance?" Bert asked innocently, breaking into laughter again.

"You—you!" Danny sputtered. "You wrote that letter!"

"Just answering your little note, Danny-boy!" Bert said triumphantly.

Danny's freckled face turned bright red. He ran over to his bicycle, jumped on it, and raced away like a rocket!

Doubling over once more, Charlie guffawed loudly. "The look on his face"—the boy gasped for air—"it was *so* funny!"

Later, when they returned to the Bobbseys' house, they found Nellie and the others waiting to hear what had happened.

Flossie clapped her hands. "It serves him right for trying to scare us about Snap!"

"He won't do that again," Nellie added.

On Saturday the twins gathered around the breakfast table a little later than usual. Nan had been glancing at the morning newspaper when she cried, "The circus is in Sanderville!"

"A circus!" Freddie and Flossie both put down their spoons. "Wowee! Let's go!"

"I wonder," Nan said, letting her thoughts drift.

"What?" Bert asked.

"I wonder if Snap's owner is connected with the circus."

Freddie's face practically fell into his cereal. "That's the worst news I've ever heard!" he said.

"He knows so many tricks," Nan went on. When her mother came into the dining room, Nan showed her the paper. "May we go, Mom?"

"I don't want to," Flossie said.

"You don't want to go to the circus?" Mrs. Bobbsey said in disbelief.

"No."

"I don't want to go either," Freddie chimed in.

"They're afraid we'll locate Snap's owner there," Nan explained.

"Oh, I see," her mother replied, gazing at the younger children. "You both know that we can't keep the dog if he belongs to someone else."

"Maybe Daddy will buy him for us!" Freddie said hopefully.

Mrs. Bobbsey smiled. "Maybe."

Her husband, however, had already left for his office at the lumberyard, so she phoned him about the circus.

"Why don't you take Snap and the children over to Sanderville this afternoon?" he suggested. "See what you can find out. I'd come, too, but I'm very busy here." He paused. "I suppose we could try to buy the dog."

"That's what the twins are hoping," Mrs. Bobbsey said.

Now that there was a possibility of keeping the pet, Freddie and Flossie were happy once again. Sanderville was several miles away and considerably larger than Lakeport. When Mrs.

Bobbsey reached the outskirts of the city, she inquired at a service station about the location of the circus grounds.

"Go straight through on Main Street," the attendant informed her. "You can't miss it. Have fun!" The children waved happily.

Traffic was heavy now, and by the time the family arrived, the show had already started. Mrs. Bobbsey parked the van and asked a guard where they could find the manager. He pointed to a small nearby tent.

Eagerly Flossie snapped a leash on the dog's collar, and they walked toward the manager's quarters as the sound of band music and applause came from the main tent.

Mrs. Bobbsey stepped into the office ahead of the children. The smell of stale cigar smoke hung in the air as they watched two men talking. One of them was short and paunchy with a fat unlit cigar in his mouth, while the other was dressed like an elegant black bird, in a black-sequined jumpsuit with feathers on the shoulders. Seeing Mrs. Bobbsey, the man with the cigar came forward.

"Are you looking for me?" he asked pleasantly, glancing past her. "Bob!" he exclaimed in amazement. "Where did you come from?"

"Bob?" Mrs. Bobbsey repeated as Snap whined and strained at his leash.

"This is Bob, Red Rankin's trick dog. He got away one night and we thought he must've been hurt or killed on the highway." He looked at the Bobbseys. "Are you from around here?"

"We're from Lakeport, Mr. uh—" Mrs. Bobbsey said.

"The name's Tiny Hayden. I own the circus."

"We found him near our house," Bert put in.

"Humph. We were traveling around the state all summer. This is probably the closest we've been to Lakeport. I wonder if Bob walked there all by himself," Mr. Hayden said.

"His name's not Bob. It's Snap!" Flossie protested. "He followed us home, and he lives with us!"

Mr. Hayden walked over to the dog and put out his hand, letting Snap lick it gently. Then Snap jumped up and put his front paws on the man's shoulder.

"It's Bob, all right, honey. He's a good dog. He and Red had a terrific act!"

"We'd like to talk to Mr. Rankin," Mrs. Bobbsey said. "Is he here?"

"Sorry. When Bob disappeared, Red's act was finished. He left the circus. I miss that redheaded son-of-a-gun. He always made me laugh."

"We put an ad in the local paper," Nan said.

"Well, no one here saw it."

"But you must know where he went!"

"Don't you worry about Mr. Rankin. He was getting tired of circus life anyhow." Mr. Hayden pulled out some folding chairs. "Please, sit down," he said.

Taking a seat, Mrs. Bobbsey sighed. "What shall we do about the dog? Leave him here?"

The circus manager lit his cigar and took a long, deep puff. "Your children seem very fond of Bob," he said. "I imagine he'll have a good home with you. Why don't you keep him for now?"

The children were greatly relieved. "Thank you very much," Nan said.

Mr. Hayden took another puff. "And if I hear from Red Rankin, I'll give him your address, so you people can work the problem out between you. How does that sound?"

"Terrific!" Nan exclaimed.

Snap seemed to approve of the arrangement also. He pranced about and let out a contented howl.

"How about staying for the rest of the show— on the house?" said Mr. Hayden.

"Thank you, but no," said Mrs. Bobbsey, sensing that the children just wanted to get Snap as far away from the circus as possible. "We'll come to see the show next summer, when you return here."

As everyone was walking back to the van, Flossie threw her arms about the shaggy dog. "I hope Mr. Rankin has gone to the moon and never comes back to get you!" she said as Snap whimpered happily.

Once more, Mrs. Bobbsey threaded her way through the city traffic toward Lakeport. Then, as if from nowhere, a small green truck turned onto the highway in front of her. She put on the brakes and slowed down. The truck swayed a moment, but finally picked up speed and raced along the road.

"That's him!" Nan shrieked. "That's the guy who was parked at school the day the statue was stolen!"

▪ 7 ▪

The Red Connection

"What's the license number, Bert?" Freddie asked, peering at the truck through the windshield.

"Can you drive faster, Mom? We have to catch that man!" the older boy exclaimed.

Mrs. Bobbsey pressed down on the gas pedal. But the faster she drove, the faster the truck seemed to go. Suddenly it careened into a side road. Mrs. Bobbsey was going too fast to turn safely.

"Mother!" Nan sank against the car seat. "You've lost him!"

"Not yet I haven't!" Mrs. Bobbsey said, entering into the spirit of the chase.

She backed into the side road quickly, turned, and sped down it. The road, however, was narrow and full of potholes, making the van bump and rock from side to side.

Finally she slowed to a crawl. "Now we *have*

lost the truck," she said, clamping her hands over the steering wheel. "I just can't go any faster on this road. There are too many ruts."

In spite of the twins' protests, she swung back to the highway. As they neared the outskirts of Lakeport, Bert asked to stop at police headquarters. "I'd like to see if Chief Mahoney has any more news for us."

While Mrs. Bobbsey and Snap waited in the van, the four children went into the building. Upon seeing them, Chief Mahoney smiled. "Do you have some more clues for me?"

Immediately Freddie told about the panel truck they had seen on the highway. "He was going so fast, we couldn't catch him!" the little boy said, ending his story.

"Very interesting," the chief said. "My men have been watching the Nelson place, and Perry isn't there. They talked to the neighbors and found out that he had planned to take his vacation while Mr. Nelson was in Europe."

The police officer continued, "We've also had a report that a gang of art thieves from New York has been operating in this area. I'm inclined to believe that the man who stole Mr. Nelson's statuette was a member of that gang."

"Do you think he has left Lakeport?" Bert asked.

"By now I'd say yes. We've sent our report to

the New York police and hope they'll have news for us soon."

Discouraged, the twins were convinced they were not going to be able to solve the mystery of the missing snake goddess after all.

"I'll let you know if we find out anything," the chief called after the twins as they left.

"This has to be the toughest case we've ever had," Bert commented, getting back in the van.

"What happened?" his mother inquired.

"Zero," Freddie replied as the engine started to hum again.

"Not zero really," Nan said. "More like sub-zero." She related what Chief Mahoney had told them.

When they were home again, Snap bounded into the backyard while everybody went inside. But a short time later Bert wandered to the back door and gazed out.

"I wonder what Snap has in his mouth," he said. "He's holding something in his teeth and running around the yard in circles!"

"Let's see!" Flossie exclaimed, dashing outside, followed by the others.

"It's only a piece of red cloth," Freddie said. Suddenly Snap dashed to the back of the yard, skidded to a stop, turned, and ran back, the red cloth flying in the wind. He shook it with a growl, then raced off again.

"Catch him, Bert!" Nan cried.

The next time Snap raced past the twins, Bert reached out and grabbed his collar. "Steady there, old boy!" Bert called.

With his ears pricked up and his tail wagging, Snap permitted Bert to take the cloth from his jaws. It was a large square of paisley-patterned red cotton.

"It's a bandanna!" Nan exclaimed. "Where do you suppose it came from?"

His fun over, Snap stretched out on the grass, panting. Dinah, who had been watching the excitement from the door, came outside.

"Do you know whose this is, Dinah?" Bert asked, flashing the big handkerchief.

The housekeeper shook her head. "Well, it's not mine. It most likely belongs to that man who was here."

"What man?" Nan inquired.

Dinah explained that while the twins were gone a man had come to the back door asking for work. She had sent him to the Bobbsey lumberyard. "I told him to talk to Sam," she said. Dinah's husband, Sam, was Mr. Bobbsey's foreman. "He was a nice-looking man with thick red hair."

"Red hair!" Bert exclaimed, glancing at his sister. "Do you suppose he's the guy from the circus, Red Rankin?"

Nan gaped. "Lots of men have red hair," she said. But then she looked worried. "Do you think he was here hunting for Snap?"

"He didn't mention a dog," Dinah noted.

"Even so, he may have come to Lakeport after he left the circus," Bert said. "Mr. Hayden did say he was going to look for some other kind of work."

"And you believe he dropped the handkerchief and Snap recognized it," Dinah said.

"Right. And now that he's got the scent, he wants to find him! I guess we've got to see if he did go to the lumberyard."

Mr. Bobbsey's lumberyard was located on Lake Metoka, at the edge of Lakeport, not too far from the Bobbsey house. The four children set out at once, along with Snap.

Snap stopped now and then to sniff at a leaf or patch of grass.

"Perhaps he's picked up the scent of Red Rankin!" Nan said.

When they finally reached the lakeshore, Snap leapt in the direction of the lumberyard. But before reaching it, he turned again and bolted to the Bobbseys' boathouse, where he stood by the door, whining.

"Red Rankin must be inside!" Nan exclaimed.

"Oh, this is 'citing," Flossie cried, taking her sister's hand.

Bert shoved the door open, and Snap dashed in. He ran to a corner where an old blanket lay.

"Nobody's here!" Flossie said, disappointed.

"Where did the blanket come from?" Nan asked. "I never saw it before!"

"Snap seems to recognize it!" Bert replied. "Maybe it's Red Rankin's."

The dog pushed the blanket with his nose. Then he ran from the boathouse onto the dock and stood there yapping.

"The man must be near here," Bert concluded. "Let's keep looking."

The twins ran along the shore, peering around the other boathouses, but saw no one.

"Let's just go to Daddy's lumberyard," Flossie suggested to the others. "Maybe he's there!"

Mr. Bobbsey was just coming from his office when the children ran up to the small building. "Hi, kids!" he called. "What are you doing here?"

"We're looking for Snap's owner," Freddie said. "Did he come here?"

"Tell me who he is, and I'll answer the question," Mr. Bobbsey said teasingly.

The children told him the story of their trip to Sanderville and about the man who had come to their house looking for work.

"Red hair, huh," Mr. Bobbsey said thoughtfully. "I did see a red-haired man talking to Sam. Let's ask him."

But the foreman could give little information. He said someone had asked about a job, but when told there was none, he had refused to leave his name and address.

"Then we can still keep Snap," Flossie said gaily, climbing into her father's car for the trip home.

"It sure looks that way," Mr. Bobbsey replied. "What do you think, Snap?" The dog sat forward on the back seat and barked in consent.

The following Monday, when the older twins were leaving school, Bert pulled Nan aside. "How about walking with me to the Nelson house? I'd like to find out if Ernie Perry is the truck driver we saw."

"All right," Nan agreed, dashing off to tell Freddie and Flossie their plan.

In a moment Bert and Nan set out for the Nelson house. It was about a mile from the school, on a shady street where all the houses were old and large and set back from the sidewalks on spacious grounds.

"I think this is where Mr. Nelson lives," Bert said. He stopped in front of a tall colonial frame house that was surrounded by a magnificent lawn and an iron fence. A driveway at the side led back to what had been a barn and was now an oversize garage. It was closed.

"What do we do?" Nan asked, trying to ignore the lump in her throat.

"Ring the doorbell and ask if Mr. Perry is in. That's all," Bert said firmly.

The two children unlatched the iron gate and walked confidently up the path to the front door. There was an old-fashioned bell in the middle of the lacquered door, which Bert twisted.

Hearing the loud ring inside, Nan jumped.

"Calm down," her brother said. They waited a moment, but no one came to answer.

"I guess the police are right," Nan remarked. "No one's here."

"Let's look around a little before we leave," Bert suggested.

The twins circled the house. All the windows were shut tight, and the shades on the second floor were down.

"Come on, Bert," Nan said. "We're not getting anywhere. We might as well go home."

The children let themselves out the gate and hurried down the sidewalk. But Nan paused to look back one more time.

"Bert!" she gasped. "There's someone at that upstairs window!"

■ 8 ■

More Riddles

Instantly Bert glanced up. "I don't see anyone!" he protested.

"Look there—where the window shade is raised!" Nan pointed. "He's gone now, but I'm sure I saw a man watching us!"

"Whoever he is, I don't think he wants us to know he's there," Bert said. "Let's go home and call the police. Maybe they'll be able to get him to open up the door."

But when Chief Mahoney called Bert back that evening, he had nothing to report. "My men can't just break into the house," he said, "much as they'd like to see if something is going on there."

The next afternoon was the puppet show at school. Bert and Nan hurried to a basement meeting room, along with Nellie and Charlie, to set up the puppet stage. Mr. Carter had put a long table on the platform that stood at one end of the room.

"Dinah hemmed this for us," Nan told Nellie as she pulled some purple cloth out of the bag she and Bert had carried to school at noon. "It'll hide us from the audience while we're working the puppets."

"It's great," Nellie said, helping Nan tack it to the edge of the table.

Bert and Charlie had made a stage out of cardboard, which they set on top of the table. Then Bert brought in four low stools from the kindergarten room.

"We can sit on these," he said. "Even if we have to crouch a little, it'll be better than squatting."

Nan gazed around. "We're all set except for the music. I'll ask Mr. Carter to get the record player."

It wasn't long before the dismissal bell echoed through the halls and the sound of footsteps rippled down the steps.

Nan smiled as Charlie eagerly collected the admission tickets from their schoolmates. "And now," she announced a moment later, "here are those world-famous Lakeport Puppets!"

"Yea! The Lakeport Puppets!" the audience cheered.

Quickly Nan took her place behind the table,

and the four little figures popped up on the stage.

There was the clown in his red-and-white suit, the blue-coated policeman holding a tiny club, and the ostrich with her rhinestone collar and long eyelashes that fluttered as she bobbed her head. Last came the cuddly white kitten.

All the puppets made deep bows. Then the kitten and the ostrich disappeared, leaving the clown and the policeman onstage.

The policeman addressed the audience first. "Do you like riddles?" he asked in a deep husky voice.

"Yes! Yes!" the children shouted.

Cupping his tiny hand around his mouth, the policeman pretended to whisper. "I'll ask this clown if he knows the answers to these."

His listeners giggled.

"Now, sir," the policeman said to the clown, shaking his stick, "what has a face but no head, hands but no feet, and runs all the time?"

The clown put his hands up to tap his head. Then a card with the word *clock* printed on it appeared behind him.

"Clock!" the audience exclaimed.

The clown repeated the word in a squeaky voice.

"You heard that!" the policeman objected, beating the clown on the head with his club.

The audience shrieked with laughter.

"I'll give him another chance," the policeman said. "When is a boat like a heap of snow?"

The clown repeated the question and again tapped the side of his head.

Again a card appeared over his head. It said *When it is adrift.* Once more the audience called out the answer, and the clown repeated it. The policeman seemed to be beside himself with anger. He paced up and down, shaking his stick and muttering.

Then he stopped and turned to the audience. "Once more!" he said. Facing the clown, he said very slowly, "What animal took the most luggage into the ark?"

Another card rose up behind the clown which said, *The elephant took a trunk.*

This time the policeman did not give the clown a chance to speak. He hit him on the head and dragged him off the stage.

Loud cheers and applause followed. The clown and the policeman popped up again and bowed deeply. When the clapping died down, they disappeared and the ostrich and the kitten sprang up.

"Meow!" the kitten said. The little children in the audience giggled. "My friend Miss Ostrich would like to sing for you!"

Bert, who had slid out from behind the table

71

and taken a seat in the front row, got up and started the record player. The melody of a familiar folk song floated out over the audience.

Nan, who was working the ostrich puppet, made her sway to the beat of the music. On the high notes the ostrich would fling back her head and open her wings wide.

Danny Rugg, who was seated in the front row, crossed his legs and hit the edge of the platform accidentally, causing the needle to skip and lose part of the song.

Flustered momentarily, Nan forgot to move the puppet, which made the audience laugh. Then Danny kicked the platform on purpose, and the needle slid over the record more.

"Please don't joggle the platform, Danny," Bert said. "You're spoiling everything!"

"I can't help it if your old platform is rickety!" Danny answered rudely as Bert reset the needle.

However, as the song continued and the singer reached a high note, Danny joggled the platform again, making the needle jump off the record entirely.

Mr. Tetlow, who could see the troublemaker from the back row, strode forward. "I suggest you leave," he said briskly to Danny.

The audience fell silent as the boy got up and stalked out of the room. Then the ostrich and kitten put on a little dance, which drew more

applause. At the end, the clown and the policeman reappeared, and the four little puppets did a bouncing jig before taking their farewell bows.

When the applause had stopped, Mr. Tetlow stepped to the platform. "We are off to a good start in raising money for our school museum!" he announced.

There were cheers and whistles as the principal went on. "I want to thank those children who worked so hard to make this program a big success. Come on out, everybody."

Still holding their puppets, Bert, Nan, Nellie, and Charlie stepped in front of the table.

"Hooray!" the audience shouted as the puppeteers bowed. "Hooray!"

"You were really great," Flossie said to the older children after everything had been packed away.

Nan hugged her little sister. "Thanks," she said.

"I'm glad Mr. Tetlow made Danny leave," Nellie remarked. "He's the biggest pest I know."

To their surprise, the boy had hung around, waiting for the children to come outside.

"You think you're so smart," he said to Bert, mounting his bicycle. "You'll be sorry!"

"I didn't do anything to you," Bert answered defensively.

"Don't pay any attention to him," Charlie advised, watching Danny ride away.

"See you tomorrow!" Bert called as his friend departed with Nellie.

When the twins reached the Bobbseys' house, no one was there. "Where is everybody?" Flossie asked.

"Mother had to go to a meeting, I know," Nan replied, "but Dinah should be here."

Just then they heard the back door slam and ran to the kitchen. Looking very worried, Dinah leaned against the counter.

"What's the matter?" Nan asked.

"Was Snap at school with all of you?" came the reply.

"No, why?"

"Then I don't know where he is! He has been gone all afternoon!"

"Snap's gone?" Flossie wailed. "Maybe Red Rankin came and took him away!"

"When was the last time you saw him?" Nan questioned the housekeeper.

Dinah dropped into a chair and began fanning herself. "He was in the backyard after lunch. And then the next thing I knew, he wasn't. I called and called. I've been out hunting for him."

"Let's scout the neighborhood," Nan suggested. "Maybe he's playing with other dogs."

Nan and Flossie went one way while Bert and Freddie went the other way. There was no sign of the shaggy white dog anywhere.

"I can't understand why he would run away," Nan said when they all had met again at the house.

"Remember, he ran away from the circus," said Bert.

"You're right," Nan said gloomily.

"Maybe he went to the boathouse!" Freddie cried.

"That's a thought!" Bert started off on a run, pulling the others along.

When they reached the boathouse, it was empty. The blanket still lay in the corner, apparently undisturbed.

Tears trickling slowly down her cheek, Flossie said, "I'll never see him again!"

"Don't say that," Nan said. "He'll come back. I'm sure he will."

Later, when their parents heard the story of Snap's disappearance, Mr. Bobbsey telephoned the police and reported the missing dog.

"If Snap doesn't come back in a day or two, we'll put an ad in the paper," he promised the children.

They tried to remain hopeful, but before going to bed, Bert and Nan made another tour of the neighborhood. As they had expected, Snap was still nowhere in sight.

The next afternoon, when school was over, Bert told his friend Charlie about the dog's mysterious disappearance.

"I'm going to look for him on my bike. Do you want to come?" Bert asked.

"Lead the way," Charlie said brightly.

For an hour they went up one street and down another, searching for Snap. Then Bert noticed a boy he knew standing on a corner and rode toward him. Quickly he described Snap. "Have you seen a dog like that around here?" he inquired.

"Hmm. Sort of. But a kid had him on a leash. He went in that house over there." He indicated a pale-yellow frame house with black shutters at the end of the street.

"That's where Danny's friend Sneaker lives!" Bert exclaimed.

▪ 9 ▪

Double Discovery

After thanking the boy, Bert pedaled back to Charlie, who had been waiting for him farther up the street. Bert told Charlie what the boy had said. "And the house he pointed to is Sneaker's!" he said angrily.

"I'll bet Danny and Jack took Snap!" Charlie declared. "Let's go get him!"

The two boys parked their bicycles in front of the Westleys' house and rang the doorbell. Mrs. Westley answered.

"Jack's out with his new dog," she said, smiling, when Bert asked to see him.

"Oh, Sneaker has a new dog?" Charlie inquired. Upon hearing her son's nickname, Mrs. Westley bristled, making Charlie shift uneasily from side to side. "Where did he get it?"

"He bought him from a friend at school," she said coolly.

The boys thanked Sneaker's mother and hurried away.

"The 'friend' was probably Danny!" Bert muttered.

"Let's ambush Sneaker!" Charlie proposed as they hopped on their bicycles again. "We can hide behind those bushes across the street and grab Snap when they walk by."

"Okay!"

At the moment, the street was deserted. They rode across to a clump of shrubbery in front of an empty house and hid the bicycles carefully. Then they crouched behind the bushes, where they could still see both ends of the street clearly.

The two detectives had been there only a few minutes when Charlie whispered, "Here they come now!"

Less than a block away were a boy and a large white dog. "That's not Snap!" Bert groaned, observing the short-haired terrier.

"I hope Sneaker doesn't catch us hiding here," Charlie said.

Their classmate was paying no attention to anything except his new pet. Whistling to the dog, he ran around to the side of the house and vanished. Cautiously Bert and Charlie got on their bicycles and rode off.

"We're not too far from the Nelson house," Bert said. "I'd like to take a ride over there. Maybe we'll get a look at the face in the window that Nan saw."

"Sounds spooky! But nothing scares me!" Charlie answered bravely.

In a few minutes they were in front of the old house. Bert gazed up at the windows. All the shades on the second floor were down. Then he glanced at the garage.

"Look! The garage door's open, and I think there's a small green truck inside!"

"The same one that was parked at school?" Charlie asked excitedly.

"I'll let you know in a minute!" Bert jumped off his bike and began to walk up the driveway.

When he reached the garage, he took out his pocket notebook and compared the license number of the truck with the one he had jotted down at school. It was the same!

He sped down the driveway to Charlie. "I have to call Chief Mahoney. Perry has to be the man we're looking for. I just hope he doesn't leave before the police get here!"

"I'll stay," Charlie volunteered, "and watch the garage. If he leaves, I'll follow him!"

"Good!" Bert jumped on his bicycle and pedaled off at full speed.

There were no stores in the immediate area,

but in a few minutes Bert found a pay phone at the corner of a gasoline station and pulled in.

When Bert had given his report, the police chief said, "I'll send Officer Murphy and another man right over."

His pulse racing, Bert sped back to where he had left Charlie. No one was there. Then he heard a *psst!*

"Bert," his friend whispered loudly, "I'm over here!" He beckoned from behind a large maple tree.

Bert hurried toward him. "What happened?" he asked.

"Nothing. I figured I'd better get out of sight," Charlie explained. "Someone might see me watching the house."

"The police will be here any minute. Then we'll find out if Perry is inside."

No sooner had Bert finished talking than a police car rolled to a stop on the other side of the street. Two officers got out—followed by Nan, Freddie, and Flossie!

Seeing Bert's surprise, Nan smiled.

"We had to pass right by your house," Officer Murphy told Bert. "I decided that if we're going to capture anyone, your brother and sisters should be in on it. So we stopped and picked them up."

Bert grinned at the other children. Then he

asked the policeman, "Now what do we do?"

"You all stay here on the sidewalk while Selby and I go up to the house," Officer Murphy directed. "I don't want you in any danger."

The twins and Charlie watched as the police officers strutted up to the door of the old house. They rang the bell firmly several times without getting any response.

Then Officer Murphy pounded his fist on the door. "Open up! Police!"

Suddenly Flossie shouted, "There goes someone!" She dashed up the walk to the two officers. "I just saw a man run away from the back of the house. He's in the garage!" she cried, panting.

By this time the other twins had caught up to her. Motioning them to stay behind, the policemen started toward the garage. As they approached the former barn, there was a roar, and the truck started to roll back.

"Halt!" Murphy shouted, running behind it.

At the sight of the policeman blocking his path, the driver leaned against the wheel, then climbed out, his face apple-red.

"What are you trying to do? Get run over?" he blustered. "I've got a right to leave this place if I want to!"

Officer Murphy called the children. "Have you seen this man before?" he asked them.

"Yes!" they chorused.

"We saw him at school," Nan said. "He tried to run over our dog."

"What's your name?" the officer asked the man.

"Ernest Perry. I work for Mr. Nelson, who lives in this house," he said defiantly.

"Where is the statuette you stole from the school?" Murphy continued.

"I don't know what you're talking about."

"Open up the truck," Officer Murphy said.

With a glare at the officer, Perry unlocked the back of the truck. "Go ahead!" he snarled. "Look all you want! You won't find anything!"

The two officers looked inside the truck. Except for a small supply of rags, it was empty.

"Satisfied?" Perry hissed. "I told you there wasn't anything in there. I don't know why these brats are picking on me."

"I guess I was wrong," Bert said.

"He could have stashed it somewhere," Nan said.

Suddenly Bert got an idea, and he whispered it to Officer Murphy.

"You're right, Bert!" the policeman exclaimed. "I don't know why I didn't think of that!"

He motioned to the other officer. "Come on, Selby," he called. "We've got work to do!"

▪ 10 ▪

Gum Giveaway

Officer Murphy stepped close to the truck. "Help me pry up this floor," he said to his partner.

Ernie Perry gulped. "You can't do that!" he protested. "You'll ruin my truck!"

"Okay," the policeman said. "If you don't want us to do it, then you do it!"

Still grumbling, Perry pushed two concealed buttons and lifted a portion of the truck's floor. Beneath it was a space filled with packages.

One by one, the police officers began to remove them until there were six bundles on the grass next to the driveway.

"Is the snake goddess there?" Nan asked hopefully.

"We'll see!" Murphy picked up a brown paper bag and peered into it, then handed it to Bert.

He opened it quickly. "It's the statuette!" he cried happily.

84

"I know valuable art when I see it," Perry boasted. "That's the best thing Nelson ever bought! It belongs to him. I didn't take it for myself."

"Are you telling us that you were planning to return it?" Selby questioned, giving the man a steely glance.

"What's in the other packages?" Flossie piped up eagerly.

While the children watched with interest, each of the bags was opened. All contained Greek art objects. There were two vases. One of them was like the vase in the school museum collection.

"That's an amphora!" Freddie announced. He was very proud that he had remembered the name Mr. Tetlow had told the children.

The remaining three objects were ornamental gold cups.

"Those are Vaphio gold cups!" Perry said. "They were made in Crete thousands of years ago. And they are also Mr. Nelson's. I was afraid to leave them in the house with nobody home, so I carried them around with me."

Officer Murphy scowled. "I believe they were stolen from the museum in Sanderville," he said. "It wasn't a gang from New York who took their art objects. It was you!"

Ernie Perry shrugged his shoulders. "You have no proof."

"Oh, no?" Bert said, his anger ready to flare. "You put on a bald wig and pretended to be an electrician when you took the statuette from school."

"That's the silliest thing I ever heard." The suspect laughed. He took a stick of gum from his pocket and began to unwrap it nervously.

"And that's the same kind of gum wrapper Freddie found in the museum room!" Flossie declared.

Perry glared at the girl.

"And here's the wig!" Freddie cried.

The little boy had climbed into the truck and searched the corners under the floor. He held up what was left of a bald wig!

"I guess that's proof enough," said Officer Murphy. Perry slumped to the ground, too weak to stand. "Help him up, Selby."

"We'd better make sure you don't go any-where," the second officer said, taking Perry's arm as he stumbled to his feet. He advised him of his rights, then took a pair of handcuffs out of his pocket, fastened one end to Perry's wrist and the other to a support in the doorway of the garage.

"I told you I . . . I didn't do anything wrong." The prisoner trembled.

"How did you expect to dispose of all of this?" Murphy questioned.

The prisoner looked at the twins and the evidence that had been collected against him. "If these kids hadn't snooped around, we'd have done all right," he said.

"Who's we?"

"A friend of mine out west. That's where the museum is that wanted the stuff." He glowered at the children. "But you had to mess everything up."

"We wouldn't have if you hadn't been so mean to our dog, Snap!" Freddie replied.

"Your dog, Snap!" Perry said scornfully. "You mean the mutt that tried to attack me?"

"He didn't attack you!" Nan retorted.

"Well, anyway, that was Bob, Red Rankin's trick dog."

"How do you know that?"

"I used to work for the Hayden Circus before I came here. That dog never liked me, and I never liked him either!"

Officer Murphy nodded to the other policeman. "Selby, let's put these things in the trunk of our car and take them down to headquarters with Mr. Perry here."

Bert looked pleadingly at the policeman. "I wonder if I could take the snake goddess back to school. After all, I'm responsible for it, and I'd like to see it safe in the museum."

The officer patted Bert on the back. "You've

done a good job catching this fellow. Take the statuette. I'll explain to Chief Mahoney."

Bert's face shone. "Thank you, Officer Murphy!" he cried. He rewrapped the little figure in the paper and placed it carefully in the basket of his bicycle.

"Could you take us to school, too?" Flossie asked as she, Freddie, and Nan climbed into the police car.

"Oh, could you? I'd like to see Mr. Tetlow's face when Bert presents the snake goddess!" Nan chimed in.

By this time Bert and Charlie had ridden off on their bicycles. "We'll take Perry to headquarters first, then drive you children to school," Officer Murphy said, pulling away from the Nelson house.

A while later, when everyone had finally gathered in front of the school building, Bert glanced at his watch. "I hope Mr. Tetlow is still here! It's after five already."

To the children's delight, they found the principal working on some reports when they walked in. He looked up in surprise.

"Well, what brings you to school at this hour?" he asked, taking off his glasses.

Bert's voice shook with excitement as he spoke. "We've brought the statuette!" He laid the package on Mr. Tetlow's desk.

"You have? How wonderful! Where did you find it?"

As the story of Ernie Perry unfolded, the principal said he was absolutely astounded. "So it *was* Mr. Nelson's employee after all!" he exclaimed. "Of course, he would know the value of the museum pieces!"

"And he was the phony 'lectric-light man!" Flossie put in.

Mr. Tetlow smiled. "Without you twins, and you, too, Charlie," he said solemnly, "I doubt if we could have recovered the statuette so quickly. I'm very, very happy to have it back."

"May we put it back in the museum?" Nan inquired.

"By all means. I'm sure Mr. Carter will take extra special care of it!"

Once again the little figure was placed on the shelf in the museum room.

"Am I glad that mystery is solved!" Bert said as the children left the building.

"Now all we have to do is find Snap!" Flossie added.

"And his owner," Nan reminded her, making Freddie wrinkle his nose in disapproval.

"So long as he lets us buy Snap," the little boy said, waving good-bye to Charlie.

Later, when the Bobbseys were seated around the supper table, Bert told his exciting story.

"I'm very proud of all of you," Mr. Bobbsey said when his son had finished. "You solved the mystery of that stolen statue and saved Mr. Tetlow from a great deal of embarrassment. Just imagine if he had had to tell Mr. Nelson one of his prize possessions was missing—"

As he spoke, a shrill whistle interrupted. Everyone stopped talking and listened. Then two more whistles came.

"It's a fire!" Freddie shouted, springing up from his chair.

As the others jumped, too, they heard the clang of fire engines rushing down the street. Bert ran to the window. A flare lighted the sky.

"It looks like it's near the lake, Dad!" Bert said.

At once Mr. Bobbsey dashed to the telephone and called the firehouse. A moment later he turned back to his family.

"It's our boathouse," he said grimly. "It's on fire!"

"Your boats, Dad, and my canoe will be ruined!" Bert cried, dashing out the door.

"I'll put out the fire!" Freddie exclaimed. "I'll get my fire engine!"

"Just a minute!" Mr. Bobbsey called. "It's too dangerous!"

"Oh, please, Dad!" Nan begged. "It's *our* boathouse, too!"

"They can stay in the van with me, Dick," the twins' mother said.

Mr. Bobbsey relented. "We'll all go. You may be able to help, Bert. The wood in our boathouse has been treated and will resist fire for a little while anyway."

As everyone got into the van, the streets started to fill with streams of people hurrying toward the lakefront. Then another fire truck sped past, its siren blasting as the glow in the evening sky reddened.

"Hurry, Daddy!" Freddie urged.

His father drove as fast as he dared through the growing traffic. But no sooner had they left a busy intersection than the Bobbseys heard a loud *crash!*

The hook-and-ladder truck that had just passed had hit something!

Frantic, Mr. Bobbsey stopped the van and darted into the street. He could see the fire engine clearly. It had struck a parked car and skidded across the street, blocking it completely!

"We have to get to the fire!" Freddie cried.

By now the firemen and several passersby were surveying the wreck. The rear bumper of the car had caught under the front of the fire truck, and the driver could not move!

"We may be able to jiggle the car out from under the truck," Mr. Bobbsey told the firemen.

At his direction two men stood on the bumper while he and two others yanked the car loose, freeing the truck at last.

Waving their thanks, the firemen hurried away to the lake. The Bobbseys followed. But when they reached the waterfront, the children gasped. Not only was the Bobbseys' boathouse on fire, but several others were ablaze as well! The wind had increased, and red sparks crackled high in the smoky sky as water from three engines poured onto the flames. Throughout, the firemen worked furiously, hacking through windows and spraying chemicals onto fuel tanks to keep them from exploding.

Now and then a hissing sound would erupt and more white smoke would billow forth from the boathouses.

Recognizing Mr. Bobbsey as he ran forward, one of the firemen said, "I hope you don't have any boats in there. The fire's pretty bad!"

"There are three of them," Mr. Bobbsey replied, looking toward the entrance. "The fire seems to be mostly on the left side, though. Maybe I can save one of the boats anyway."

"Let me go with you, Dad," Bert said, catching up to his father. "I'll be careful."

The fireman didn't want to let them pass, but they burst past him. At the same time, Sam and another man from the lumberyard joined Bert

and his father. "We'll get the big boat out!" Sam cried.

"Okay," Mr. Bobbsey said. "Bert and I will see about the rest."

Quickly the men ran the larger launch out into the lake while Mr. Bobbsey jumped into his motorboat and started the engine.

"Paddle down the lake!" he yelled to Bert, who was already in his canoe. "Pull in at the first dock. I'll meet you!"

Suddenly, to Bert's horror, the wall next to him began to cave in!

▪ 11 ▪

A New Catch

Hearing the sound of burning wood, Bert paddled fast and hard until he reached the welcome cool air of the lake. He wiped his moist forehead shakily and let out a long sigh of relief.

As he rowed past the boathouse next door, a large spark fell into the canoe. It landed on a cushion that had been left in the bow, and began to crackle.

Instantly Bert put his paddle on the bottom of the canoe, and holding on to the gunwales, inched his way forward. The craft rocked from side to side, causing him to sway. But finally he stretched out one hand and grasped the edge of the burning cushion and tossed it overboard!

"Whew!" Bert blinked his eyes.

A few minutes later he joined his father and

the two lumbermen at the dock. They had tied up their boats and helped pull Bert's canoe onto the shore.

Mr. Bobbsey gave Bert a hug. "Good work," he said, gazing back at the yellow flames.

When they returned to the others, the crowd was silent.

"Where's Freddie?" Mr. Bobbsey asked his wife.

She pointed toward one of the fire engines, where Freddie was talking to the fire chief.

"Freddie!" Mr. Bobbsey called. "Leave the man alone. He's busy."

The fire chief took Freddie's hand and led him back to the others. "We've been having a nice chat," he said. "By the way, was anyone in your boathouse this afternoon?" he asked Mr. Bobbsey.

"Not that I know of. Why? Did the fire start there?"

"Looks like it. My men examined the place the minute they got here. They found a partly burned blanket in one corner. Someone could have dropped a lighted match on it."

"I haven't used any of the boats for several days," Mr. Bobbsey said. "Perhaps some prowler broke into the boathouse."

The same thought on all their minds, the

twins looked at one another. Had Red Rankin set the fire?

Before anyone could speak, however, the chief produced a battered-looking book. "Ever see this before?"

Bert gasped. It was a geography textbook! "Where did you get this?" he asked.

"We found it right outside your boathouse."

"May I look at it?" Bert asked. He took the book and opened the cover.

"Whose is it?" Nan inquired.

Her brother held the book under a nearby streetlamp. "It's Danny Rugg's!" he exclaimed. "Hmm. I wonder how his book got here!"

"There's Danny now!" Flossie blurted out as she pointed to a group of boys standing around one of the fire engines.

"Ask him to come over here, will you, Bert?" the fire chief directed. "I want to talk to him."

Bert strode toward Danny and Sneaker, who were talking to another fireman. When Bert relayed the chief's message, the freckle-faced bully twitched nervously. "Why does he want to see me?"

"He found your geography book outside our boathouse," Bert said. "He—"

"I don't know anything about it, and I'm not going over there!" Danny said rudely.

He turned to flee, but not before Bert had

98

reached out to stop him. Danny shoved him hard, making Bert trip over a fire hose and fall backward.

"Get out of my way!" the bully snapped angrily.

Nan had seen everything and started forward as Danny ran off. "Catch him!" she cried as her twin struggled to his feet.

"We'll get him!" Freddie and Flossie shouted, racing after Danny. Bert and Nan joined in the chase.

The next minute Danny stumbled over a hose himself and fell to the ground with a thud.

"Listen," Bert said when Danny stood up again, "it's not going to do you any good to run away. The chief wants to talk to you, and if you don't do it, he'll come after you."

The other boy hung his head. "I'll go back," he said.

Soon he was standing face to face with the fire chief. "Is this yours?" the chief asked Danny quietly, holding up the geography book.

"I don't know anything about it," came the somber reply.

"It has your name on it," Bert said.

"So?"

"I told you it was found by our boathouse," Bert continued.

Danny looked worried but said, "For all I

99

know, you took the book and put it by the boathouse yourself!"

"Watch it, young man!" Mr. Bobbsey warned.

Under further questioning by the fire chief, Danny finally admitted that he and Sneaker had been in the Bobbseys' boathouse just before suppertime.

"Where is your friend?" the chief inquired.

"Sneaker!" Danny's sharp cry rang out loudly, drawing the second boy to his side.

"Now, tell me, young man," the chief said, his eyes glued to Sneaker, "what exactly were you two boys doing in that boathouse?"

For a few seconds there was no reply. Then Danny spoke up defiantly. "We were looking for clues!"

"Clues!" Bert said in amazement. "To what?"

"We thought maybe we could find that old statuette," Danny said. "Sneaker and I are just as good detectives as you are!"

Flossie giggled. "The snake goddess is back in the school museum, Danny!" she exclaimed. "Bert found it this afternoon!"

The boy looked downcast but said nothing.

"Did you light any matches while you were in the boathouse?" the fire chief continued. Sneaker glanced at Danny but did not answer. "Tell the truth."

"Maybe we did light one or two," Sneaker ad-

100

mitted finally. "But we didn't start the fire!"

"It probably hadn't started when you left," the man explained. "However, if a match landed on that blanket before the flame was completely out, it may have smoldered there. Eventually the blanket set fire to the boathouse!"

Danny and Sneaker trembled. "We—we didn't mean to hurt anything!" Danny stuttered.

"Maybe not," the fire chief acknowledged. "But even so, you're old enough to know that it's dangerous to play with matches! Get into my car over there!"

"Wh-what are you going to do to us?" Sneaker asked.

"I'm going to take you both home and explain to your parents what has happened. It'll be up to them to punish you!"

When the boys had left, Flossie climbed into the van with the other three children. "I'm glad our boats didn't burn up," she declared.

"Maybe I really will be a fireman someday," her twin said blissfully.

Just then they heard loud barking.

"What's that?" Freddie asked as a shaggy white dog leapt out of the bushes and into the glare of the headlights. "Snap!"

At once the children tumbled out of the van. Flossie threw her arms around the dog.

"Oh, Snap!" she cried. "Where were you?"

Snap wagged his tail, pranced on his hind legs, and barked again.

"Isn't he funny?" Freddie said.

But then the dog stopped and bolted toward the woods.

"Stop him!" Nan shouted. "He's going away!"

Snap barked again, then looked at the twins mournfully and ran toward the woods once more.

By this time, Mr. and Mrs. Bobbsey, flashlight in hand, had joined the children. "I think he wants us to follow him," their mother said.

"I think so too," Nan agreed.

With Mr. Bobbsey in the lead, the group walked into the woods. Farther and farther they went, following the dog, who trotted at an even pace.

"I hope he knows where he's taking us," Mr. Bobbsey said.

At last Snap halted, running around in circles and sniffing at the ground.

"Now where's he going?" Nan asked as he struck off toward the lake.

Just as she spoke, the dog gave a yelp and bounded forward. A short distance ahead was a man seated on a rock by the water.

"Hello there, Bob!" he said, pulling the dog's ears affectionately. "I'm glad to see you— thought you'd run away again!"

Then he heard the footsteps behind him and jumped up. When he saw the flashlight beam and the six onlookers, he looked startled. Mr. Bobbsey introduced himself.

"And—and I'm Red Rankin," said the other man, his hair giving off a coppery glow in the flashlight.

"Mr. Hayden at the circus told us about you," Bert put in quickly.

"Did you happen to use a boathouse to sleep in?" Mr. Bobbsey asked suddenly, thinking of the blanket that had been found.

"Yes, I did, but I'm sure I didn't cause the fire!"

"Perhaps we'd better go back to the van and discuss everything."

"Were those your boats in there?" Red inquired.

"Yes, but we got all of them out safely," Bert said.

"Well, I'm glad to hear it." On the way to the Bobbsey house the circus man explained that he had had very little money when he left the circus. "I came to Lakeport hoping to find a job. I wandered down to the lake and figured I'd spend my nights in one of those boathouses until I did."

Fear growing in his eyes, he looked at Mr. and Mrs. Bobbsey. "I was very careful not to disturb

103

anything, and I never lighted any matches. I had no reason to. You've got to believe me. That fire wasn't my fault!"

"Don't worry, Mr. Rankin!" Mr. Bobbsey said in a kindly voice. "We know who caused the fire, and it wasn't you."

"But when did Snap find you?" Freddie asked impatiently.

"Snap? Who's Snap?"

"We named your dog Snap," Bert explained. "We hope you don't mind. We didn't know what his real name was."

"Oh, that's all right." The man laughed, relaxing, as the children explained how the dog had followed them home from school.

"He wanted to stay with us all the time," Flossie said.

"Well, I can see why. You seem to be real nice people."

It wasn't long before everyone had reached the Bobbseys' house, where Dinah threw open the door and practically leapt down the front steps.

"I've been so worried about you! Is the fire out? Sam came home an hour ago!"

Then she saw Snap. "Where did you find him?" she asked, shaking the dog's paw. "Welcome back, Mr. Snap!"

Now Flossie took their visitor's hand and introduced him. "This is Mr. Red Rankin," she announced. "Snap belongs to him," she added sadly.

Dinah peered at the man. "How do you do?" she said. "Weren't you here the other day looking for work?"

"Yes, I was." He laughed sheepishly as Mr. Bobbsey led the way into the living room. "I think we should sit down and talk a little," he said.

The twins' mother added, "Dinah, I think we could all use something hot to drink. All of a sudden I feel rather chilly."

"Coming right up," Dinah said, bustling toward the kitchen.

Freddie and Flossie followed her. There, in breathless detail, they told the housekeeper about the miraculous rescue of the boats, the discovery of Danny Rugg's geography book by the burning boathouse, and how Snap had suddenly appeared and led them to Red Rankin.

"My, my, you've had quite a night!" Dinah exclaimed.

"We sure have!" The little twins laughed gaily.

They helped her carry in cups of steaming cocoa and a big plate of homemade cookies. As Mr. Bobbsey took a cup, he addressed Red Rankin.

"Suppose you tell us about yourself," he said.

Speaking in a soft, low voice, the trainer said that after his trick dog had disappeared, he had stayed in Lakeport, hoping to find the dog and rejoin the show.

"But I couldn't locate Bob," he went on, "so I started looking for any kind of work. Then yesterday I spotted Bob by your boathouse!"

"He knew you were around here because you dropped your bandanna in our backyard," Nan said. "We had heard you were heading to the lumberyard, and Snap picked up your scent in the boathouse."

"We were with him, but we couldn't find you," Bert added.

"I didn't spend too much time in the boathouse," Red explained, taking a sip of cocoa.

"What are your plans now?" Mr. Bobbsey asked.

Red Rankin looked uncertain. "Frankly I don't know. I was just offered something with a construction company," he said.

"That's great," Mrs. Bobbsey remarked.

"They want to send me to Central America. To tell you the truth, I'm a little tired of circus life. I'd really like to try something else."

"If you go to Central America," Bert said with some hesitation in his voice, "will you take Snap—I mean Bob—with you?"

Red gazed at the dog, now lying contentedly in front of the children. "That's a tough question," he said.

As he pondered the answer, the twins thought about the exciting events of recent days. How long would it be before they had another mystery to solve? They would find out when they discovered *The Mystery at Snow Lodge.*

"I'd like to buy your dog," Mr. Bobbsey said, breaking the silence. "We're all very fond of him."

"Well, Bob and I are old friends," Red replied. "I'd hate to part with him. But"—he glanced at the forlorn faces around him—"I'd be glad to let him stay in such a good home."

"You would?" Nan cried. "Oh, thank you! Thank you!"

Freddie and Flossie jumped up and threw their arms around the man while Bert shook his hand.

"Snap is ours!" Freddie exclaimed joyfully. "Hooray!"

"Now that we know his name, will we have to call him Bob?" asked Flossie.

"Bob Bobbsey?" said Dinah mischievously as she appeared in the doorway. "That's *really* too much. I think Snap is a good name after all."

MICK. Born a blue-eyed son, a life in his close-knit Irish community has already been mapped out for him. But what if it's a life he has no stomach for? Can he tear up the map and throw it away?

SULLY. He's always been Mick's best friend. He's always followed Mick's lead. But now their checkerboard neighborhood is changing, and Mick is moving off the white square of home—into dangerous territory. Should Sully follow? Does he really want to?

EVELYN. She's beautiful and she's a poet. She's also hard as nails. Mick can't resist her—probably because he's the last thing in the world that she wants.

TOY. He's street-smart and worldly-wise, and nobody messes with him—ever. Mick can't believe how lucky he is to have Toy as a friend. And then he begins to learn some of Toy's closely guarded secrets. . . .

TERRY. Mick's big brother is a violent drunk, and an even more violent bigot. In fact, he's the local hate monger. Lately he's been hating the fact that Mick doesn't want to follow in his footsteps. . . .

Also by Chris Lynch

Shadow Boxer

"A gritty, streetwise novel that is much more than a sports story." (Starred review)

—School Library Journal

"The fight sequences, fraternal dynamics, and memorable cast of eccentric characters make for some riveting episodes in this rough, tough-talking book about boxing and brotherhood."

—The Horn Book

Iceman

"Much better than the usual sports novel, this is an unsettling, complicated portrayal of growing up. . . . A thought-provoking book guaranteed to compel and touch a teenage audience." (Starred review)

–ALA Booklist

"Hockey enthusiasts will enjoy the abundant on-ice action, although this novel is clearly about much more. . . . *Iceman* will leave readers smiling and feeling good."

—School Library Journal

Gypsy Davey

"The dialogue crackles with realism . . . in terms of literary quality, this work is outstanding." (Starred review)   —*School Library Journal*

"Young adults will appreciate [*Gypsy Davey*'s] honesty and fast pace. Lynch steers clear of sensationalism and paints characters who ring true every time."

                    —*Bulletin of the Center for Children's Books*

dog eat dog

Blue-Eyed Son #3

CHRIS LYNCH

HarperCollins*Publishers*

Excerpt from "Travel" by Edna St. Vincent Millay.
From *Collected Poems,* HarperCollins.
Copyright 1921, 1948 by Edna St. Vincent Millay.
Reprinted by permission of Elizabeth Barnett, literary executor.

Library of Congress Cataloging-in-Publication Data
Lynch, Chris.
  Dog eat dog / Chris Lynch.
    p.   cm. — (Blue eyed son ; #3)
  Summary: Blinded by his hatred for his sadistic brother, Mick
challenges him to a dogfight.
  ISBN 0-06-027210-4 (lib. bdg.) — ISBN 0-06-447123-3 (pbk.)
  [1. Brothers—Fiction.   2. Family problems—Fiction.
3. Dogfighting—Fiction.]   I. Title.   II. Series: Lynch, Chris.   Blue eyed
son ; #3.
PZ7.L979739Do   1996   95-34691
[Fic]—dc20   CIP
                                                                        AC

Typography by Steve M. Scott

First Edition

Contents

Sully's Gift

My life had come to seem to me like a combination deal. As if I were at the beach and there was a wicked undertow *and* I didn't know how to swim, so I couldn't get out of the damn water to save my life. My sadistic brother, Terry; my neighborhood; my parents—my parents owning a bar was like Jack and Mrs. Ripper running a cutlery shop. These were the undertow, the factors I could not alter, that would hold me down forever if I didn't break loose.

But the no swimming part, that was me. That was nobody's fault but mine. I finally got a date with Evelyn of my dreams and I showed up wasted. Who was to blame there? Sully, who turned out to be more reliable, more loyal than I ever realized, who turned out to be more friend than I deserved, Sully and his family took me in when I couldn't go home again. I said thank you by setting their house on fire. Who would I blame for that? Terry had gotten me so twisted up with hate that I began acting just as disgusting and ignorant as he did in an effort to prove I was better than he was. More than once already I'd flashed on the thought that I could kill him, without regret, if that would settle everything for good.

And Toy, who was there so many times when I needed him. Toy, to whom I was running one more time for a solution. What did I do for my friend Toy?

She was his mother, for chrissake. Why couldn't I hold that thought when I needed to? What is the matter with a person who acts the way I do? And is it curable?

These were the thoughts that swirled through my head as I lay where I did not belong. But they all instantly shrank away next to the size of my new problem. My own father was medium big, and Sully's father was scary big, but when my eyes opened and Toy's father, Carlo, was standing beside me casting a shadow over me and Felina and the nightstand, my fibrous little body went rigid as an ice pop. That's what I must have looked like to him too as he whipped back the covers to expose us naked on his bed. Felina was cool, waking up gradually, stretching and purring, coiling back up again all curve and caramel on the white sheet. I was her opposite, petrified, laid out straight as a number 1.

He was a hairy mountain of a guy, with a black beard and a black leather cap, and when he spoke it made the bed vibrate.

"Who we got here, Lina?" He didn't sound all that concerned about it.

"Company, Carlo." Neither did she.

As I lay there waiting on my fate, the two of them chatting across my body, I found out something about myself. When I get totally, out-of-my-mind terrified, I get a furious erection. Right there, like a centerpiece, it sprouted into the middle of the conversation. Which probably didn't help anything.

Carlo grabbed me by the hair. Again not angrily, but with a growly sense of determination.

As I was leaving the bed, I did not know what was going to become of me. But for one instant, it didn't matter. I reached out my hand on the way by, lightly placed it flat on the smooth, buttery skin of Felina's belly, and let my fingertips

3

ski across her, as he pulled me away. Just to save it, to keep it all for a bit.

"Say good-bye to company, Lina," Carlo said as he hauled me out. She waved.

Carlo yanked pretty good as he towed me along. It hurt, and I was scared, but I was grateful. Whatever he did to me, I was still glad it was the husband, and not the son, who found me.

He dumped me, nude, on the sidewalk in front of the house, then went back inside without bothering to beat me. Felina whistled from the window, dropped my stuff down, and disappeared again. Three people walked by one at a time and none seemed to notice me dressing on the sidewalk.

I was at the O'Asis, my parents' bar. I was supposed to be working, but I was sleeping at a table, holding my mop. The tapping at the front window woke me. It was really more of a porthole, and made of green bubble glass, so you couldn't tell who was out there. I opened up anyway.

"Those the clothes you were wearing Saturday?" Sully asked, holding his nose. "Change before you go to school, will ya? And where did you sleep last night?"

I looked at my clothes, only now realizing that I'd been wearing them for two days straight.

I wore them to bed when I set the house on fire, wore them to Felina's, and put the same rags back on while standing on the sidewalk. All this while carrying several changes of fresh clothes right there in my bag.

"I didn't sleep last night," I said. "I had a lot of adrenaline, so I walked instead." A smile came to me as I recalled it, where I got that adrenaline. Once again, I had lost track of the point, that it was Toy's *mother* I was celebrating. Sully was a gift, showing up here, now. He was the only one I could tell, and I couldn't wait.

"So, how was *your* weekend . . . ?" I began slowly.

By the time I'd meandered my way to the point of the story, Sully's mouth was hanging wide open. I reached over and closed it up for him.

"You did *what*?" he asked in a desperate whisper even though we were the only ones in the place.

"I—"

"You did *what*?"

"I said, I sl—"

"You did *what*? You did it with *who*?"

I let him answer himself now. All I could do at this point was giggle anyway.

"Jesus, Mick, what are you gonna do? I mean,

5

congratulations and everything, but what are you gonna do?"

I held for a second, then exploded, jumped right up out of my chair. "I think I'll . . . climb the Matterhorn, swim the English Channel, wrestle an alligator. . . ."

"I think *that*'s gonna happen sooner than you think, bub."

"I want to do it all. Today. C'mon, Sul, let's go tip over some Subarus, right now."

Finally, he caught some of my enthusiasm as I flailed around, dancing with my mop as I cleaned the floor. Sully lightened up some, but still he was concerned.

"Ya, maybe we can tip a couple on the way to school, but we have to get going. To *school*. You remember school, dontcha, studley?"

I started mopping much more slowly as things began coming back to me. Damn, school. School seemed so . . . small now. Then something bigger occurred to me. Where do I go *after* school? I'd traveled a million miles the last couple of days and come back to find the same old problems, only worse.

Now it was my turn. "What am I gonna do, Sul?"

He walked to me, took my mop away. "First, you're gonna change your clothes."

"But I mean later. Where am I gonna go?"

"You're gonna come home with me, right?"

"What's that, a joke? You gotta know what happened."

"Ya, I know," Sully said, picking up the mopping where I'd left off. "But he said you could come back."

I had already half stripped, and was pulling fresh clothes out of my bag behind the bar. "Your dad? He said I could come back?"

Sully waved me off like I didn't know anything, which was turning out to be pretty true. "He ain't nowhere near as mean as he makes out. As a matter of fact, he said he never actually threw you out in the first place. He was just a little angry about you burnin' his house, went downstairs to get his gun, and when he came back you were gone."

I was at the sink, splashing water into my armpits. "Jeez, sounds like I overreacted then, huh?"

"Ah, he wouldn't've shot ya. Just woulda waved it around and yelled a little," Sully laughed. Then he got a shade more serious. "Truth is, you owe me for this one. *I* got him to let you back. I kicked his ass. . . ."

"Excuse me?"

"Did I say kicked? Sorry, I meant kissed. I

kissed his ass to let you back. And it tasted like shit, too, so you better appreciate it."

I did. And he knew I did, so I kept my back to him, stayed at the sink washing and grinning to myself. This may have been the only thing that could have pushed Felina out of my mind for a minute. Sleeping back at the Sullivans' again was suddenly more exciting than sleeping anywhere, with anyone, else.

"The kicker is that you don't have your own place anymore, Mick. You're banned from the attic. Gotta stay with me now. That okay?"

This time I turned around dressed and some-what cleaned. "Ya, Sul," I said. "That okay."

"Cool. Listen, we're gonna be late, so let's wrap it up. What's left to do?"

I pointed to a bucket of rags and Tilex, then pointed to the bathroom. "You do in there. I have to scrape the floor back here."

Bravely, Sully went into the bathroom. There was a three-second beat, and he came back out again, gasping. "Oh my *god*," he said, marching behind the bar and handing me the bucket. We switched jobs. "One of these days you've got to stop shittin' on me, Mick," he grumbled.

By the time we got to school, Sully had relaxed. But now I was tense.

"Somebody's *mother*, Mick?"

"Shut up."

"Okay, let me put it another way: *Somebody*'s mother."

It was an excellent point. Toy wasn't just big, and tough, and a pretty serious guy. There was something unknown about him, that you didn't *need* to know, to realize you didn't want him mad at you. And there was the other thing, the rightness of him. You knew he'd never do something like that to somebody else's mother, and that was what stung even more.

I swallowed hard, a loud gulping swallow. I had to just go about my business, like any other school day, that's all there was to it.

Automatically, I went to Evelyn's homeroom and waited outside for her.

"This one too, Mick?" Sully said, gesturing inside to where Evelyn was already seated. "Jeez, once you start, you're an animal, aren't ya?"

He was just a buzzing in my ear as I stared at Evelyn from the side. She looked neat and proper and all smart again, as far away from me as she was back at the beginning. I felt a huge acidy hollowness spreading in me as I watched her, and I felt stupid for being there. She must have felt me watching, because then she turned.

As Evelyn got up and came my way, Sully

moved away at the same speed, as if they were two opposite magnets.

"Hello," she said.

"Hello," I said, thinking this was a nice start.

She shook her head. "How do you feel? Are you sick at all?"

I toggled my head around, taking stock, getting a feel for myself. "No, I'm okay. Thank you for asking."

"That's good. I have to go to class now."

"Wait," I said. "Ah, about that y'know, mistake I made . . ."

"That's far enough, Mick," she said. "We don't have to have this talk. You're a decent enough guy, I think, way down in there somewhere. But you have a lot of work to do. You have . . . *problemas. Tu sabes?* We're not talking about a mistake. We're talking about things that are deep in you. As of right now, we're not quite right for each other. Maybe later. Okay?"

She reached out and grabbed my hand, pulling the fingers apart like breaking a wishbone. I hardly felt it.

"Mick? Mick, your face doesn't show me anything. Are you okay?"

"I'm okay," I said, though I wasn't. This should not have hurt me at this point, should not have surprised me. But it did, and it did.

She seemed, from her expression, as if I had spooked her. She waved Sully to come and get me. "You'll be fine," she said as Sully came up from behind and grabbed my shoulder. "Summer is almost here, and that's going to be a new world. The summer is refreshing, the summer is hope. You never know, with the summer. We'll see, Mick, okay?"

Somehow, through the powerful weirdness of my confusion, I had turned her. Sully was ushering me away and Evelyn was staying there in the hallway, talking to me. "You just take it easy, Mick. Let's take it as it comes, all right? We'll talk. You rest. Summer will be good."

Sully pushed me down into my seat. "Well, that went well," he said. As soon as I sat down, the bell rang to get up. Eight thirty, and I was already totally wiped out.

I managed not to see Toy until lunchtime. When I did, as he approached my table in the caf with that long, slow stride, I heard something build like a tympani drum roll in my ears. It was my heart.

"Hey," he said as he sat across from me and Sul. I said hey, then stuck a spoon in my mouth and started chewing it. At least it would keep me from swallowing my tongue. Toy stared down at me. I couldn't see the eyes. I knew the angle of

11

the hat by now, and the stare was withering me. Sully kept kicking my ankle, for laughs.

"My old lady said you were looking for me," Toy said.

"Ya, I was, lookin', I was lookin', lookin' for ya, Toy, I was lookin'," I babbled, the spoon still in there.

Sully decided to help me out.

"So, how *is* your mom, Toy?"

"She's none of your damn business, Sullivan. Thank you for asking."

Sully didn't help me anymore.

"Your date didn't work out so well," Toy said.

"Huh?" My hands were shaking, so I sat on them. My eyes were about to spill with fear tears.

"Your date. I heard about it. You went down in flames with Evelyn. Sorry to hear it. You, ah, regressed, I believe."

I nodded. Nodded involuntarily with my whole jangly body.

"Are you sick?" Toy asked, tilting his head to get a better look. I shrugged.

"Anyway, you wanted to talk to me."

"C-c-can we do it later, Toy?" I asked, excusing myself from the table.

"Not a problem," was the last thing I heard before I fell. My knees buckled, my legs all water from nervous exhaustion. Toy rushed over just ahead of Sully to pick me up.

"I'm okay, I'm okay," I said, and Toy let me go. "I think I'm gonna go see the nurse. Sully, you want to take me home?"

"I'll catch up with you later," Toy said, and it sounded to me like a line from an old gangster movie.

Sully hopped up enthusiastically, taking me by my elbow like I was an old person. I shook it off, he grabbed it again. I shook it off, he grabbed it again, laughing. "Finally," he said, "finally, I get to see a benefit from being your caretaker."

Honorary

The Sullivans seemed to like me better after I burned their house. They really adopted me after that. Anyway, I didn't actually burn the place, just the one wall in the one room. My room. But not anymore.

I still spent a lot of time there, though. Every chance I got, slithering up the stairs to just sit on the floor and stare out the dormer window, kind of like a private church thing for myself.

"Yo, Buddha, you comin' down to eat?" Sully called from the bottom of the stairs.

I pulled myself away reluctantly. I could stay up there for hours, pretending it was still mine, but I couldn't miss meals with the Sullivans.

"I still don't get this, Sully. Why am I treated better around here now?"

"It's my mother. She can't resist a cripple. She's always putting up stray animals and loser relatives for weeks at a time. Every year on Labor Day, she gives, like, thousands of bucks to Jerry Lewis, the whole weekend, just keeps calling back and pledging more and more, until Dad has to yank her out to a movie and dinner. She's a sucker, big heart stuff."

Though there didn't quite seem to be a compliment for me buried in there anywhere, I liked the explanation anyway. I could fill the injured animal role, if someone really wanted to fix me. I ate with them, like I did every night now, listening to small talk about people I mostly didn't know. I listened to Mr. Sullivan rail on about all the idiots in the world, including, in great detail, my own family and myself, as if I wasn't right there to hear it. He just didn't care, which I admired.

Pot roast, mushy soft potatoes and carrots in cocoa-brown gravy. When I finished working my bread, you could have put the dish right back in the cupboard, it was so clean.

"Ah, clean plate club," Mrs. Sullivan chirped.

"Duh, Ma," Sully said.

I laughed. How stupid, how wonderful.

I went with the whole family into the living room. Mrs. Sullivan sat at one end of the couch. I sat next to her. Sully rushed up, wedged himself between us.

"You stay away from my mother, you animal," he whispered in my ear.

"You are so low," I said.

"What?" Mrs. Sullivan asked, smiling, as if this was a joke she would actually like to be let in on. I just shook my head.

Mr. Sullivan stretched out on the floor, flipped on the TV. "You're in for a treat, Mick. It's a very special cinematic event we're going to be sharing with you here."

The three of them started laughing at once. I was lost. Felt kind of eerie.

The film came on. *The Fighting Sullivans.* It was a based-on-fact World War II movie about five brothers who served on the same ship in the navy. In the end they all croak together except one.

"We always fight ta-gedda. We always fight ta-gedda," Sully squawked, mimicking a character from the movie.

"A *giant* of a film," Mr. Sullivan crowed. Within sixty seconds, he was snoring.

The movie was hysterically sappy and lame, but that wasn't the point. They'd obviously done this a thousand times before, Sully trading off with his mother, spouting dialogue and laughing, Mr. Sullivan even wafting in and out of consciousness for the occasional remembered line. I watched them all as much as I did the movie, sneaking long looks at the sides of their faces. An hour into the movie, Mrs. Sullivan joined her husband in sleep, her face resting lightly in her palm, her elbow propped on the sofa arm.

Sully looked at me, which he hadn't done until we were alone. "Goofy, huh?"

"Ya," I said, with admiration.

"Well, it's sort of official now, you've been adopted. You've been made an honorary Sullivan."

"Ooooh," I cracked, too stupid to act honest yet. "Oh, *that'll* open some doors for me, huh?"

"Stop bein' an asshole, Mick."

He kept staring into me. Very un-Sully.

"Okay," I said.

That was the good part of what came from my big weekend. Out of the fire, more or less. The Sullivans took me in. Took me deeper than before, and that was nice. Strange as hell, but nice. Who could figure? I couldn't figure that. Family stuff, who could ever figure?

The not-so-good part was Toy pursuing me.

"You wanted to talk to me?" He was at my locker.

"Ya. But I gotta run, Toy."

"You wanted to talk to me?" He was in gym, aiming a white leather ball at my head.

"Gotta run," I said about a quarter-step too slowly. The gym teacher, who was also the school nurse, gave me an ice bag for my nose.

"You wanted to talk to me?" He was sitting in front of the superette, smoking a long thin cigar.

"Ya, but jeez, Toy, now I completely forgot what it was about. I'll catch ya—"

"Now. You'll catch me now, Mick." He had a grip on the back of my shirt, pulling me down to sit on the milk crate next to his. He held up a cigar, and I took it.

"Acting pretty damn weird lately, Mick."

I nodded, bobbing my head in and out of the smoke cloud that hovered in front of me. "*Feeling* pretty weird lately, Toy."

"Hmmm?" he said coyly. "You mean, like, guilty?"

"Ahhh." I inched my crate away as I spoke. "Maybe, maybe guilty is it, I don't know. It's a lot of things, feels like every kind of feeling in me all at once." I watched him out of the corner of my eye to see if he knew, if he was guessing, if it was just coincidence. I could see nothing.

I was so scared, when I pulled the cigar out of my mouth I sneaked—for the first time in many years—a little tiny sign of the cross, drawn with my thumb tip across my lips. If I was going to be dead in a second, I wanted my grammar school God right there with me. Toy scared me in a lot of ways, more than Terry and his friends and their attack dogs and all the rest combined.

"Why'd you do that?" He'd caught it.

"I had a little tobacco spit on my lip, that's all."

"Funny shape for a spit," he said.

We paused, smoked.

"What's it about, do you suppose . . . your guiltiness?"

"I didn't say I was guilty, exactly."

"You done something you shouldn't have? Something *bad*?" He exaggerated the word *bad*, mocking it, as if he didn't believe in it.

"Nope," I said, steely.

"Yes you did," he said.

I waited. I even closed my eyes for it. The only good thing was that Toy was *so* tough that I'd probably be dead before I felt anything.

"I heard you set Sullivan's house on fire. True?"

I let out a very, very loud *pheewww* sound, like the sound of a fire extinguisher. That was all he knew?

"Ya, ya," I said happily. "Practically burned a whole wall down."

"What are you, proud? I would have killed you. Did the old man kill you?"

"No. He threw me out, though, but then he let me back in."

"He took you . . . ? Mick, can I tell you that I don't understand the way your neighborhood works *at all*? Can I tell you that? Myself, I'd have *killed* you. Would have torn your lungs right out if you did something like that in my house."

I accidentally inhaled the cigar smoke. Coughing, coughing, hacking, I felt my whole head get flushed. My lungs felt like they were tearing, but at the moment it was good to feel them still in there.

"You all right?" Toy said, beating on my back hard.

I nodded, slowly regained my breath. The feeling of Toy's big hand covering most of my back relaxed me, took away a lot of the fear. When I stopped being afraid of him, I felt a need to talk to him.

"I almost left, you know. I packed my bag and left the Sullivans' without even knowing where I'd go. Just wanted to once and for all bolt from this town."

He nodded. He relit his cigar.

"But I didn't leave."

"But you didn't leave." Toy said it as if there was no other possible end to that story, like, *of course* I didn't leave.

"Why didn't I leave? I still don't have a real answer to that. I look around and I can't see why I'm here. So . . . ?"

He nodded again, as if I had said something to agree with.

"You understand, I know it, Toy. Let's talk about you, for example."

"Let's not," he said with the cigar clenched in his teeth.

"No, really. You go on trips all the time. And you always come back."

Very slowly he drew the cigar out of his mouth. "One time I won't," he said quietly.

"Where do you go, Toy, on your trips? Huh, where do you go?"

He stuck the cigar back in his mouth and talked around it again, turning away from me at the same time. "Mick, did I tell you a long time ago that it was none of your business where I go? I don't remember, did I tell you that?"

"Ah, ya, I believe you did, now that you mention it."

"Good, so I don't have to tell you that now."

"I guess you don't."

Toy stretched out, groaned, stood to go.

"Wait a minute," I said, panicky. I needed to get something from him. Something. "The reason I asked is that I think maybe I should start by doing what you do, you know, just taking regular trips instead of leaving for good yet. Do you think?"

"I think you already take regular trips, is what I think."

"Don't say that. I'm straight now. I'm not wasting myself anymore."

Toy put his hands on his hips and spat the stub of the cigar out in my direction. "Just like that?"

"Just like that. That was the first step, to not be a fuckup anymore. The next step is to be more like you. You just have it all together. I want that."

"Okay, you want it?" He growled the words at me. "The story is that you are like me. I'm a fake, and so are you. Just because I don't tell you things about myself doesn't mean I'm not lying at the same time. And you, all you want, Mick, is to bingo-bingo, snap your fingers and change into something you think is cool. But you know it didn't work. Dressing up like Ruben didn't deliver you. Hanging with me, chasing Evelyn, that didn't deliver you. Running away from here wasn't going to deliver you either and at least you finally realized that, that you were just going to carry your crap along with you.

"Problem with you, Mick, is you think you're a better guy by changing your clothes or your address. You think your disease is in the leaves, when it's in the roots."

I couldn't look at him now, so I stared at his boots. Funny, when Carlo threw me out with no clothes on, I didn't feel like I was naked in the street, but now? Now I felt naked in the street. I always figured this, that Toy knew a lot about a lot. I just never should have asked.

"Mick, don't pout. That's another thing you need to quit. Stop acting like the victim all the time. Get on with it finally, will you please? I'm happy to help you out, if I can, but it gets hard after awhile to be patient with you."

I tried hard to stop pouting, but I could feel the face still there. It wouldn't go away while Toy was in front of me.

"I'll see you tomorrow," Toy said, his timing as fine as always.

Mickey the Dog

Get on with it, Mick. Disease in my roots. Victim all the time. Just going to carry the crap with me. Wherever. Get on with it finally, will you please?

Finally, it was clear. Finally, *something* was clear to me. I had to kill the disease.

"Mick, phone," Mr. Sullivan boomed. He shook his head.

"Family?" I asked.

He nodded and grinned.

"I want you to come for dinner." It was my mother.

"No."

"Please? For me."

"Um . . . no."

"Mick, you cannot continue this way for-ever."

I did know that. Finally. I had come to that conclusion. "Is he going to be there?"

"He really wants to see you, Mick. He says as much every single day."

"I'm not coming, Ma."

I could hear her fingers drumming on the telephone table. "Well . . . what if Terry wasn't here? Would you come then?"

"I might. Are you saying he won't be there?"

She hesitated. "I'm saying that, yes. Will you come?"

I got a little morbid thrill out of the thought of going back there. But also, I had a need, a con-dition that needed treating.

"I'll be there."

Half an idea. When I got myself together for din-ner at my parents' house, I did it the way I did everything, with half an idea. I knew I wanted to look good, to look like I was successful and not needy, but I didn't know what I wanted to look like. I knew I wanted to stuff it in Terry's nose, that I got some of what I got from him, but I didn't want to come in wearing the evidence. So I didn't wear any of the clothes I stole from him, but I went clothes shopping with the money I stole from him.

I stood at the door wearing shiny black Doc Martens, the ugliest footwear of all time, but an item they could all recognize. I wore a red silk shirt buttoned to the collar, brown Levi's 554 baggies, a huge black satin baseball jacket, and matching Chicago White Sox cap. Tiny oval sunglasses that barely blacked out my eyes.

My father answered the bell.

"Told ya he'd wind up selling drugs," he called over his shoulder to Ma.

She slapped him on the shoulder. "Mick, you look very sharp," she said, and gave me a quick shoulder hug. She took my jacket, hat, and glasses as I sat at the table. I hadn't even warmed the chair yet when she started serving. She buzzed nervously around, rushing to the kitchen and back, slapping mushy vegetables, mushy mashed potatoes, mushy boiled ham onto plates. "You look very healthy, you look very nice," she jabbered.

"You look very pimp," Terry said, winging his leg over the back of a chair.

"Ma!" I called as she disappeared into the kitchen.

"Keep your voice down," Dad growled as he started peeling beers off the ring. "That what they do over Sullivans'? Scream at each other like animals?"

I waved my beer away. Terry snatched it up, nodding, his mouth already overflowing with food.

"You coming home yet, or what?" Dad asked.

"We got no room for him," Terry answered.

Ma sneaked up on her chair, slipped into it under my glare. "Of course we have room for him," she said. "We will always have room for him."

"Ya," I said. "Not that I'm coming back, but of course you have *room* for me. *My room*, remember?"

Terry shook his head gleefully. He started talking, *then* put meat in his mouth, without slowing down. "Uh-uh. Dog lives in there now."

I stared at my mother some more. When she wouldn't stop averting her eyes, I just spoke up. "I thought he wasn't going to be here," I said.

"Why shouldn't he be here?" Dad barked. "He *lives* here. Gettin' awful snotty there, Mick, lately." His voice trailed as he bore down on his food. "Goddamn Sullivan."

"Ya, Jesus, kid, don't be such a piss now," Terry said. Terry was having a fine time. "Dontcha even want to know his name?"

"Ma?" I said, trying to address my original question.

"Please, Mick," she whispered, trying not to answer it.

"Ma," I said more forcefully.

"Mick, I am his mother. Why can't you understand that? I'm his mother just like I'm yours. You might see yourselves as being two very different creatures, but I cannot. I might just as well cleave myself in two, as pretend even for a minute that I have one of you and not the other. It may not make any sense at all to you, but I just haven't got a better explanation than that."

She couldn't have been more right, about me not being able to see it. And from the barely contained laugh rumbling in Terry's throat, this was one of the few things we agreed on. But Ma did manage to shut me up with it.

"And *that* is why you have to come home," Dad said. "You're killing your mother." He refreshed his palate with a full beer.

"What about Mickey?" Terry said to Dad. Then he tipped a glance to me. "His name's Mickey. I named him for you, you ungrateful sonofabitch."

"Build a doghouse out back," Dad said. " 'Cause he can't have run of the house."

Terry turned to me again. "That okay with you, bro? You won't mind living in a doghouse? We can get you some curtains and a rug. . . ."

"No thanks, Ma," I said. "I'm set now. Really I am."

She looked down now and played with her food. Her terrible sloppy overcooked food that she always made unless she burned it. I didn't miss the food, but I could live with it, no problem. She was hurting, I could finally see, and I was surprised by that. Somewhere inside, I was pleased by that. As I looked at her, I understood I was hurting too, and I was *most* surprised by that. I would be back, I wanted to tell her, but not till Terry was out of the picture. I wasn't here because of him, and I couldn't accept that anymore.

There was nothing really left to say. Ma brought me there for that one conversation, and we were no good at anything like natural give-and-take. Dad didn't particularly care whether I was at his table or not, as long as I didn't get between him and the refreshments. All that was left, creepily enough, was the Terry dance. He stared, he bit, he drank, he slobbered, he wiped his mouth on his sleeve. He smirked at me, he winked, he coughed little pieces of food so they landed on my plate. I looked back at him, not shying away like I used to. We set it all up right there across the table, without words. A bull and a bullfighter, or just a bull and another bull. We had a date. I was either coming over to the other side, or else. . . .

"Ma, supper was great," Terry said as he got up. "We gotta go now."

"We?" she asked.

He looked down at me. "Ya."

Ma looked to me, her face questioning.

"Ya," I said firmly.

"We're gonna take Mickey for a walk."

Ma looked both hopeful and afraid, even more confused about all this than I was. Dad just waved his fork at us. "You two don't make no sense at all."

I waited on the porch while he retrieved the dog, a brown shepherd-Doberman monstrosity. It strained at the leash, wheezing in the choke chain as it pulled harder and harder, strangling itself. I hopped up and walked backward down the stairs, as I was the thing it was trying to reach.

They were perfect for each other, and the beast calmed right down when Terry addressed it. "Ain't he beautiful?" he said sincerely, making goo-goo eyes at the dog, bending down to kiss him on the mouth. It was the closest I'd ever seen Terry come to something like love.

"No," I said, because the animal was not beautiful. He was big, in a clumsy, retarded way,

and still growing. He looked strong and dangerous and about to fall over all at the same time.
Some of his hair was short and some of it was
long, like a mange pattern, and all of it was
orange, like Terry's. He had a very pointy face.

"Gotta get y'self a dog, Mick. Gotta."

"Don't gotta," I said, in his stupid voice.

He shook his head at me, waved me to start
walking. "You don't understand nothin', man,
dogs is where it's at today. A guy's dog is who he
is. Dog can *be* you, y'know? Like, let's face it,
mosta your white guys, they can't fight no more,
life's been too good to them, what with bein'
lucky enough ta be born white and all. So they're
soft. Like you. Niggers are stronger, spics are
faster, and even the gooks and the heebs—people
ya used ta be able ta count on—now even they'll
stick ya in a damn heartbeat. You get a blade,
they get a machete. You get a nine millimeter,
they get a Uzi. It just don't pay."

"No, it don't."

"You're gettin' wise wit me, boy, but you still
don't get it. This is, like, the wave of the future,
where the dogs do the fightin'. Your dog is special. You train him, you raise him, maybe you
even breed him perfect, till your dog is like a dog
version of yourself. Cunnin'. Mean. Smarter than
all the other dogs. Then he does all your killin' for

31

ya, and you don't gotta get your head knocked at all, 'cause now it's the best *dog*-man, the sharpest, that winds up on top and everybody else can just kiss my ass."

I was stunned. I could not recall Terry ever before stringing together three sentences on one subject without forgetting what he started to say. He had clearly been working on this.

"What do you get out of all this, Terry?"

He slapped his dog on the back of the head, out of anger at me. "You're so stupid, Mick. You're so ignorant. It puts things back the way they belong. It puts us back in *position*, y'know. The future of warfare. It's high fuckin' tech."

Terry's snapping at me got his dog agitated. He started straining again to get at me.

"No, Mickey," Terry yelled, yanking the chain, letting it go slack, then snapping it tight again.

"Let him smell your hand," Terry said, talking to me the same way he talked to the dog. "No, no, no, turn it palm *up*. You want it to be a stump?"

I let the dog smell me. His lip curled in a snarl as he did. I froze.

Three or four long whiffs later, Mickey decided. His ears, which had been lying back flat on his head, stood up. The hair on his long curved horse neck smoothed out too. He stood at attention beside Terry, which seemed for him to be a relaxed state.

Terry smiled. "See? He likes ya. 'Cause ya smell like me. He can smell that, your insides, that they smell like mine. Dogs know the real stuff."

I didn't take the bait. "Where are we going?" I asked calmly.

"Are you just bein' stupid on purpose, or have you been gone that long?"

When we strolled into Bloody Sundays, we were showered with *whoo-whoo-whoo*s as if Terry had the world's finest woman on his arm. "Looky look," Danny said as I took a stool beside Terry. No one even seemed to notice the dog. The bartender slapped two pints of Guinness in front of us, laughing. "You can take the boyo out of the Bloody, but you can't take the Bloody . . ."

I immediately took my beer and placed it on the floor in front of the dog, who inhaled it.

"Hey. Don't do that again," Terry said. "He has a problem."

"Where's Augie?" one of the big fat Cormacs asked Terry, adding, "Hey, Mick," as if he'd just seen me yesterday.

"I ain't seen him," Terry said. "He'll be here. Spooks show yet?"

Cormac laughed. "Think maybe you could tell if they was here or not, bro?" He gestured around the room full of puffy round faces in various grades of white and pink.

Terry laughed too. Then he gave me the rundown.

"Nigs from Mattapan, Jamaicans, are bringin' by their hot shit dog tonight, stupid shits. Gonna get his ass *whipped* tonight, for sure."

I leaned back, away from him. I pointed at Mickey the dog. "Your dog's here to fight, Terry?"

"Nah, he's just here to watch, he ain't ready yet. I want him to learn a few things. It's Bobo. These fools heard about him and came lookin' for a match. Word's spreadin' all around the goddamn city about how Bobo's thirty and 0. Like gunfighters, they're poppin' up all over."

This made Terry suddenly giggle hysterically. "We're gettin' stinkin' rich on it. *And* we get to put certain ignorant, cocky sonsofbitches in their places at the same time. Heh. Bobo's enjoyin' the shit out of it too."

I stared at Terry as he chugged heartily on his drink, slapping the bar for more while the first one was still on his lips. Staring blankly had no impact on Terry, so I was forced to talk to him.

"This is what you do now? For fun?"

"Yup. You'll see. It's a fuckin' unbelievable rush when it happens. Like nothin' else. My favorite part is watchin' the faces of the assholes who own the loser dog. They just about die. I been lookin' forward to these Jamaicans, boy. . . . I swear, I might cream myself when it happens. You'll see. You can't resist it."

"I think I probably can resist it, thanks."

He clearly didn't think that was possible, grinning sagely as he picked up his glass. He was sure we shared this animal lust on some deep level. I wanted to kill him with my bare hands, open his jugular with my own teeth. But that didn't exactly seem like the way to prove him wrong.

"He could lose, you know," I said, trying to derail him.

"Don't be stupid," he said. "Bobo? Never happen. For sure not tonight. Jamaicans love Dobermans, while your regular American spooks prefer Rottweilers. Good, mean dogs, the Dobermans, lotsa heart, but not enough body. They ain't big enough to take on the beasts, and they're too ballsy to quit. So"—he shrugged—"when they don't win, they get shredded. Kay-ser-fuckin'-ra, ser-ra."

The eight Jamaican men filed in behind their

dog—a Doberman, all right—like a military outfit. Mirror sunglasses, rigid posture, expressionless. Mickey stood up and started barking, snarly and wild barking. The Doberman didn't even look, maybe couldn't turn because of his owner's grip. Four men took spots at the bar, four more standing behind. They drank double rums and beers. Terry picked up the tab, nodding and smiling a ratty thin smile across the bar. The owner of the dog nodded and said something to the bartender, who pointed to the back door. They all filed out to the fenced-in lot in back of the building.

Slowly, others began slipping out there. The Cormacs went, and Danny, and ten of the other regulars. Terry looked at his watch. "Where is he?" Danny asked nervously.

One of the Jamaicans came in, walked up to Terry. "Time," he said.

"Five minutes," Terry said.

Ten minutes passed. The Doberman's owner came in. "What?" he said, holding out two upturned palms as if he was waiting for rain.

"Late," Terry said.

"Lose," the man said.

"Bullshit."

"Chickenshit. No show, money go. Too damn bad, mon."

"Just give us some time," Terry said.

"Got no time for you," the man said. He took a look around the bar, sniffed disgustedly. "Did have time, wouldn't waste it here anaway." Then he looked down, pointed at Mickey. "What wrong wit him?"

Terry looked down, surprised. "Him? No, not him. He's not—"

"Shit," the man said, miming as if to slap Terry's face back and forth. "Give me my damn money, boy."

Terry's face went scarlet. He sat on the stool for a half minute without so much as blinking. All activity in the bar—even sipping—stopped.

"Lead the way—boy," Terry said to the man, giving Mickey the dog a needlessly hard yank.

I didn't leave my stool. I didn't need to. When they pushed through the back door, the small crowd outside made the noise of a full NFL stadium. I could barely hear the dog noises over the din, but they did come through in a wail here and a throaty growl there. Something live crashed into the door again and again. A woman screamed an ear-shattering scream, and demanded to be let back in. But they would not open the door during the match. The men screamed until there were no more words, only primal, raked-throat squalling.

Then, of course, there was nothing. The door opened and people began silently pouring back in. The Jamaicans filed through as orderly as they had arrived, only this time with their dog breathing hard and excited, bouncing, leaving his feet, snapping at the air, licking blood off as much of his face as his tongue could reach. They took up their spots at the bar for the victory drink.

No Terry. I didn't want to see what was out there, but I had to. I got up and walked through the wake that the bar had become, and paused at the door. I was operating on some kind of animal curiosity and a foggy sense of what I *should* do, but the one thing I felt certain of was that I was going to throw up when I got out there.

As soon as I'd forced myself through the door, I slammed it behind me so as not to put on a show. But I was still only staring at my feet. Gradually I raised my eyes up and up until I hit on it.

Terry stood, hands on hips, looking down on his dog. Mickey. Mickey's head, on top of that fine horse neck, was turned around. From the look of it, the Doberman had grabbed Mickey's face, and twisted it backward. Then he got what he was after, what all fighting dogs seem to be after, the throat. As I stood mesmerized, I could see the fully exposed apparatus of Mickey the dog's throat, working up and down, struggling for one last swallow.

I laughed.

As I laughed, I listened. I heard the gurgling, the struggling for breath. I saw Terry's face. I put them together, and I laughed.

Terry twisted his face my way. His eyes became slashes, meaner and more dangerous than his drunken squint. His hands remained on his hips.

"I told you," he said through gritted teeth. "I told you you was gonna love it. I told you you couldn't resist." He pulled back and kicked the dog, what was left of the dog. He looked back at me. He looked back at the dog. He kicked the dog again while looking at me. "Inferior dog, that's all we got here. A loser."

Finally we were there, and he no longer had the advantage. He hated me as much as I hated him. I thought I was going to cream myself.

"You were right, it was great fun," I said, laughing myself into a wheeze as he sunk his foot into Mickey, laminating his good work boot with blood.

No Exit

There is no exit out of the bullring behind Bloody Sundays. It's just an eight-foot wooden fence surrounding a concrete patio. And being the strict place that it is, patrons are required to remove their decapitated animals from the premises. The bartender gave Terry an extra-large Hefty lawn-and-leaf bag for the job. He had to drag it back out through the bar.

Danny gave him a ride to the Animal Rescue League to drop it off. I rode in back next to the body. Terry was unusually pensive and silent. He didn't even say thank you as Danny passed him the bottle.

As for me, I couldn't control myself.

"Hey, ah Terry, Mickey's not looking too good back here, you think you could roll down his window a bit? Maybe some fresh air . . ."

He ignored me.

"Animal Rescue League, huh? They better have *Jesus* on the staff, if they're gonna rescue this animal."

"Shut up, asshole," Danny said.

"What? Huh? What's that you say? Well, I'll ask them. Hey Terry, Mickey wants to know if we can stop at Burger King."

"You want me to beat his ass, Terry?" Danny offered. Terry waved me off like a fly. I leaned back and laughed.

When we reached the Animal Rescue League, the scene was surprisingly uneventful. Danny pulled in the gate and turned up to the front entrance. Terry walked around to Mickey's door and pulled him out. He simply dumped the green lump right there at the curb, like he was putting out the weekly garbage.

"That's it?" Danny asked as Terry got back in.

"I ain't fillin' out no damn paperwork," Terry said, snatching the bottle back.

"Ya, all those *X*s to sign," I said. "Who needs it?"

He ignored that one too, and after that there

wasn't much to say. With the corpse gone, the ride was hardly any fun at all. I didn't see anything funny anymore, didn't feel like I *had* him now. I stared out the window.

"Back to the Bloody?" Danny asked.

"Shit no. I don't want to see that now. We'll go over to my old man's joint."

"Drop me off," I said immediately.

"Absolutely," Danny said.

Slowly, as we pulled up to the Sullivans' walk, Terry turned around in his seat. His pointy, flushed, grinning, gap-toothed face was intense and scary bearing down on me, looking just like every picture of the devil I'd ever seen.

"Don't you worry, Mick, we won't make any mess at all at the O'Asis, where you gotta clean up in the mornin' and all."

It made me gag just to think about what they could do, but I wouldn't let him win this. I got out, slammed my door, and tapped on his window.

"I might know a dog," I said coolly, "that could whip Bobo's ass."

He stared straight ahead through the windshield, not at me. "Ya, right, boy. Tell ya, Bobo has a date with a Doberman next, but after that, you just go right ahead and bring your little mutt over. We'll be happy to serve him up."

"Date." I smiled, leaning into him.

"Date." He smiled, turning to meet my face up close.

I thought about it, about Terry and the dogs and all the rest, as I cleaned up the O'Asis in the morning. Terry and Danny must have called up everybody they knew to make this much mess, because no two people could have done it. Food and broken glasses covered the whole floor. Curtains were pulled down and shredded. The bathroom, Christ, the bathroom. There was so much piss reeking up the floor and wall that they must not have even attempted to hit the bowl. There were pictures scrawled on the walls in marker—the goat, someone shoving something down a guy's throat while someone else stuck something up the guy's ass. Many barely legible and not too creative notes about me. It was like I had uncovered a hieroglyphic-filled cave from some ancient subhuman tribe.

"*Dog*fighting?" Toy said. "That's Neanderthal."

"Uh-uh," Ruben said. "My dog don't fight. My dog has a philosophy—you don't come in my yard, I don't eat your freakin' guts out. It's a pretty good philosophy, I think."

"As much as I hate to agree with Ruben," Sully said, "you have to be a loser to make your dog fight another dog. I'd just let it go, Mick."

If nothing else I had united Toy, Sully, and Ruben on the same side of something, which I never would have thought possible. The three of them sat there on milk crates one beautiful sunny day the last week of school, smoking cigars and telling me don't do it. But they didn't understand. They didn't get it. They couldn't, because they didn't have my problem.

"Hey, Mr. Sullivan," I said when I had him alone after dinner that night, "can I get a dog?"

He stopped, folded his arms. "You'll feed it, clean up after it, walk it all the time, bathe it so it doesn't stink, pay for its food, and don't let it bark?"

"Absolutely." I was thrilled.

"Hell no, you can't have a dog . . . asking me ridiculous questions like that . . ." He walked away muttering true stuff about my family.

That whole week, the last week of school, I felt something, something moving. Something moving away from me. Because for the first time ever, it was my school and not my immediate neighborhood that held things together for me. Besides the Sullivans, all the other new stuff that had happened had spun out of school. The whole Evelyn thing, even if it was a disaster, gave me a sense of purpose, of somewhere to go. Ruben changing me into a clone of him was kind of dumb, but it took me someplace new. And Toy. Seeing him at school, hanging out at the superette, getting sick on the cigars. Getting rescued by Toy. The road trip. Toy helping with Evelyn. Felina.

When school was out, was I going to go back? There? I had my plan to destroy my brother, which kept me busy, but what beyond that? It didn't help that Toy began dropping hints that he might not be around anymore once the summer came.

"What, you mean like a trip, only longer?" I asked hopefully.

"Ya, like, longer," he said.

We were walking along together after school. Off the steps, past the superette, where we didn't stop this time. We continued in the direction of Toy's neighborhood. We didn't talk about it, even though this was something we didn't normally do. At the end of the day, Toy usually split, alone, no invitations to follow. But this was June, when things were different, when something in you was lighter and you did things different. You even talked. About stuff beyond the usual stuff.

"The whole summer, maybe, you mean?"

"The whole summer, maybe," he said.

45

"I know I'm not supposed to ask this, but where are you gonna go?"

Under the straw hat, a big grin pushed his ears up, pushed the hat up.

"Home," he said, almost sadly. "I'm thinking I'm going to go home."

This seemed like a lot of information from Toy. I tried not to sound surprised. "Where's home?"

"I don't know yet," he said.

I didn't like the sound of it. It sounded far away and it sounded for real and for good.

"Anyhow," I said brightly, "you might not be going anywhere, right? We're just talkin'."

"Just talking," he said.

We were standing outside his house now. I found myself staring past Toy, up at the second-floor window.

"She's not in there," he cracked.

My stomach jumped. I tried to say something, a denial or something casual. But nothing came to mind.

Toy was unconcerned. "She's on a trip of her own this time. It's her turn. About time, too. She deserves it."

"Oh, ya, good for her," I said, acting as if she was no concern of mine. I did stop looking at the window now, though.

"I'd invite you in, Mick, but I'm not sure this house is such a good place for you."

"Yes it is," I said, and immediately felt strange saying it.

"Go on home." Laughing, he walked away.

The One Remains

I never asked, but eventually I sort of moved back upstairs into the attic of the Sullivans'. I didn't live there like before, all independent and self-sufficient and dangerous. I was still an honorary Sullivan, eating with them, watching their TV, sometimes sleeping in Sully's room, but I wasn't a *real* one. I needed the time, and the space, that the upstairs provided. They all seemed to understand—even Mr. Sullivan—and as long as I didn't burn anything they left me alone up there.

It gave me a small bit of confidence back, living up there again. Gave me just enough to try for a little more.

"What are you doing here?" Evelyn asked suspiciously, finding me outside her homeroom on the last day of school.

"Thought I'd say hi," I said. "Hi."

"Hi."

We stared at each other. Everybody walking by was happy, bouncing, whooping. Last day of school. But nobody said anything to me, or slapped my back. Nobody touched Evelyn either.

"It'll be good to be out," she said.

"It will," I said.

"Good luck," she said, and started inching into class.

"I was thinking," I said, stopping her. "That since I don't have many friends, and you don't have many friends, that we could maybe be, you know, friends, even without school. Summer, you know?"

"Wait now, there's a difference. *I* don't have friends because I don't *want* any. *You* couldn't *buy* one."

"Shut up."

Her mouth dropped wide, wide open.

"Excuse me?"

"I said shut up, Evelyn. Shut up is what I said. You know, you're not what I'd call a warm person."

A long smile fanned slowly out across her face, and I almost loved her again.

"Does this mean you don't love me anymore?" she asked.

"That's what it means."

She nodded.

"I do want to walk you home," I said sternly, feeling suddenly powerful over all this.

"That would be lovely," she said.

The end of school was uneventful like never before. The bell rang—they were letting us go an hour early, which was a big surprise since they do that the last day of every year—and I filed out into the sun of June the same way I filed out into the rain of October and the ice of February. June usually settled things for me for the year, finished stuff, started other stuff, better stuff. But now, nothing was settled.

"Where's Toy going, Evelyn?" I asked as we kicked along toward her house.

"I don't know."

"I think maybe you do. Where's he going, and why does he have to?"

"I don't know, and it doesn't matter, Mick. What's the big deal anyhow? People come and people go every single day." She threw up her hands. A casual move she didn't do casually. "Everybody gets replaced, right? Let it go."

She picked up her pace. I followed three feet behind, staring at her.

"Come on, Evelyn. Even you aren't that cold."

She turned to face me but kept walking, backward, as she recited:

> *"The One remains, the many change*
> *and pass;*
> *Heaven's light forever shines, Earth's*
> *shadows fly;*
> *Life, like a dome of many-coloured*
> *glass,*
> *Stains the white radiance of Eternity,*
> *Until Death tramples it to fragments.*

"That's Shelley," she sighed, then turned away from me again.

"That's swell," I said, letting a little more distance build up between us. "You know, Evelyn, I used to think I wanted to be like you. Now I don't think I'd like it, being you."

"No, you wouldn't," she said, slowing down finally to force me to catch up. "And neither do I."

We sat on her porch drinking Coke—me— and peach essence seltzer—her—without talking too much. The summer heat was just starting to pinch the city, and that was the thing that seemed to guide us. I sipped, she said something about the vacation to Miami she dreaded taking in July. Then we said nothing. She sipped and I talked about the Knights of Columbus Fourth of July picnic I was planning to miss for the first time since I was in diapers and my old man let me suck the sweaty foamy backwash out of brown Black Label bottles all day until we both puked. We have it on a sixteen-millimeter movie.

I told her this Fourth of July I was just going to stay home and watch the movie instead. She laughed. I smacked the first mosquito of the summer, but he had already stuck me, and he burst with a bellyful of my blood. We didn't say anything for a long time, sitting there watching cars go by, but that was fine.

"You slept with Toy's mother, huh?" she piped through the silence.

"Jesus *Christ*," I said, hopping to my feet. "Where did you hear that? Huh?"

She giggled. "It's in the girls' bathroom at school."

"Oh shit, oh shit, oh shit, oh shit," I said. "Oh shit." I paced maniacally, up and down the stairs like I was doing a Gene Kelly dance routine. "Well, it's not true."

"Come on, Mick," she said, really laughing now. "You can't tell me it's not true. It's in the girls' *bathroom*, I told you."

"Oh my god," I said, sitting down on the bottom step with my head in my hands.

Evelyn sat next to me on the step. "There's a name for what you did, you know. I'm too much of a lady to say it, though."

"Oh my god" was the best I could do now, and I was stuck there. "Oh my god."

Evelyn patted my shoulder. "Don't get so worked up."

I raised my head, hopeful for a second. "Does he know? Do you think he knows? No, he doesn't know. Does he?"

She laughed very loud now, louder than I thought a girl could laugh without being stoned. *"Yo no sé,"* she choked out. "Why don't you ask him yourself?"

"Hey," Toy said, walking up behind me and leaning with his boot up on the third step.

"Hey," Evelyn said.

"Hey," I squealed. My voice was as high as a referee's whistle.

"What's up with you two?" Toy asked.

"Just sitting," she said, "breaking in the summer. Exchanging some poetry. Want to hear?" she said, then started without his answer:

> *"There once was a trucker*
> *and an-other trucker;*
> *The first trucker turned out to be*
> *a m—"*

"Tell him the other one!" I blurted. "Um, the Shelley, um the one about Death trampling to fragments . . . no, don't tell him that one . . . do ya have anything with flowers?"

Toy reached out and gripped my arm.

"It's okay," he said, in such a warm, deep hum that I felt I could believe it. Almost.

"What's okay?" I asked nervously.

"Whatever. Whatever, it's all okay. I'm just here because I wanted to tell you guys I'll see you."

Evelyn stopped laughing. "What do you mean, Toy, you'll see us? You're leaving? Now? The school year has been over for an hour and a half, and you're leaving?"

"I'm anxious. More anxious than I knew," he said.

"But right this *minute*?"

"Well what, I should hang around awhile? So you can throw me a going-away party, have a cake, gather up all my friends for a group hug?"

Evelyn tightened her lips, so that it was hard to tell how puffy and red they actually were. She stopped talking to him.

The other stuff didn't matter to me much now. I stared up to Toy and felt like I was losing something great. And once again my mouth went to a place my brain had never dared go.

"I want to go with you," I said.

He was reasonable and gracious about it, considering we both knew I was lapping over into an area I wasn't allowed. "Nah, you wouldn't enjoy it," he said brightly, clapping me on the shoulder. "And besides, I don't *want* you."

I turned to look at Evelyn as Toy took his big foot off the step. She was shooting him angry eyes.

"I'll be back," he said without looking back at us. "I'm just going to look around right now. I'll see you again."

I turned once more to watch her watching him. The ice poet cried big hot June tears that fell in her lap. I put out my hand to catch one.

"You love him," I said.

"It doesn't matter," she said.

Hot

June got hot. Sweaty relentless life-sucking August hot. It came and wouldn't go. Things are different in the heat. There are no rules when it's that hot out for that long. You can do anything, and it seems okay.

I went to the rematch. Bobo and the Doberman. Turns out Bobo missed the first one because he stepped on a broken bottle and even though he probably could have won walking on two legs, Augie would never expose him at less than his total awesome flesh-shredding self.

Now two weeks later, Bobo was healed, and it was hot. The Jamaicans loved it hot. Their dog loved it hot. Augie and Terry and the rest of the fair-haired boys, they didn't like it hot, no way. Bobo didn't like it hot either, but that was okay because it just made him meaner. And very very thirsty.

I even invited my roommate, Sully, along.

"Hmmm, let me see now, go to Bloody Sundays, watch one frightening animal tear pieces out of another frightening animal, for the viewing pleasure of a whole group of *more* frightening animals, after which, in all probability, they will all turn their attention on skinny human prey such as, oh, say, *moi*. Jeez, Mick, it sounds damn tempting, but I think I'll stay home and ask my dad to pistol-whip me instead. But you go and have a good time anyway."

More and more it was clear that there would be no overlap. I could be here, in the safe Sully world, or there in the Bloody one if that was what I wanted, but when I crossed over, I went alone. It wasn't that I wanted to go. I had to.

"Hey boys," I said as I strolled up to the whole group of them gathered at the Bloody bar. Terry, Augie, Danny, the fat Cormacs, and Baba. Bobo and Bunky lay panting on the floor, lapping away every few seconds at a plastic washtub full of water.

"Hey boy," Terry answered, pissy for all of them. It was clear to everyone now that even though I was back, I was no friend of the court. My disrespect at the passing of Mickey the dog had given me away. Clear to everyone but Baba, that is, fresh out of detox, with a sparkling clean slate and very spotty recall. We were old friends again, there deep in Baba's head.

"Yo Bones," Baba said, slapping me crisply and warmly on the side of the head. "Come for the party, huh? Gonna be a booger bloodbath, man." He laughed.

"Ya," I said, and elbowed my way to the bar. The traditional automatic beer was not there for me as it was for everyone else. And for everyone else it was there every ninety seconds or so. This was power drinking, even by Bloody Sundays standards. The room was broiling hot with ovens blasting in the open kitchen and hypertense, overstoked bodies radiating their own noxious heat around the overcrowded bar. The one open door and two lame staggering ceiling fans were not up to the challenge.

So of course they drank. Stouts. Lagers. Black-and-tans. Like lemonade at a sidewalk stand, the brew flowed, glasses accumulating to cover the bar top. Terry's face got so red he achieved yet *another* type of scary, not scary like he'd kill you, but like if you touched his face with your finger it would burst like an overripe tomato, splattering red pulp all over the walls. Baba nodded, revived, nodded, slammed the bar. The bartender stopped serving him—a first in Bloody Sundays history. Whenever Baba asked for another beer, he received a Coke. He didn't seem to notice.

"Your friend ain't gonna make it," Augie wheezed, leaning too close to my face while pointing over his shoulder at Baba. "We thought he was gonna. Thought he was gonna be great. But . . ." He smiled a long evil grin, showing that he'd lost another tooth lately. "But he's fried. Two damn beers now and he don't know his goddamn name no more."

I shook my head solemnly. "That's a cryin' shame," I said. "When you lose one of the great talents, and so young."

Augie's mouth was hanging open, something genius about to ooze out, when his and every other head turned to catch the Jamaicans filing in. Even more than the last time, they were sharp. All in berets this time, shirts pressed, spit-shine clean and looking cool as October, they were the opposite end of everything from Terry's buddies. Like last time, they all silently sat at the bar, crisp and orderly, having their ceremonial shots. Opposite them, the Bloody's boys slobbered, sweated, postured. And shrank.

There was not a bead of sweat on the

Jamaican side. Someone, as a joke, had set an empty pint glass on the bar under one fat Cormac's chin. It was now one-third full of gray perspiration.

The murmurs started, about how badly Bobo was going to mutilate the Doberman. But they were quiet murmurs. Followed by low, vicious chuckles. Terry and Augie stared lasers across the bar at the Jamaicans, who didn't bother to look back.

"Can I get a Coke, finally?" I said to the bartender after he'd served everyone in the place at least once while ignoring me. Terry's boys exploded in a long, moronic, fear-charged laugh at me and my drink order. They were thrilled to have someone or something defenseless to turn their hate on. The racket was so shocking, in the middle of their shrinking, that it drew stares even from the Jamaicans.

I smiled back at them all. "My drink order's pretty funny, huh?" I asked as my Coke arrived with no ice. "Tell ya what, then. So youse don't think a me as totally limp, I'm gonna buy."

"Whooo," they said as a group, pretending to back away from all my power.

I turned, still smiling, to the bartender. "Shots, Stoli, all up and down," I said. This torqued it up. They barked, cheered, laughed wildly as the bartender set them all up. They went out of their minds when I added, "Screw it, sell me the bottle, man."

He dead fished me, bubble eyed and more stupid than he had to be. "Pay me for the god-damn round."

Both Terry and Augie spoke up at once. In their perverse way, they were impressive and overwhelming. "Sell him the fucking bottle," they growled, even if that bartender was their father, protector, god, long into almost every night. Like dogs lying in the midday sun, it didn't matter to them who got in between them and what refreshment they needed. They'd shred him.

"Twenty-five bucks, you little underage shit," the bartender sneered.

I pulled out the money. "And give me a bag a them chips. No, not them, the salt-and-vinegar ones. The big bag."

More noise, more wild woofing. The bartender refilled their glasses and gave me the bottle. I laughed with them as they tossed the drinks back and slammed the glasses on the bar. I tore open the bag of chips, and dropped it to the floor under the bar where Bobo devoured it.

Terry and Augie laughed harder as the Jamaicans calmly stood and filed out the back into the bullring. The others—Danny, the Cormacs—drank their last shots more slowly. Double gulping, not really shooting. They held their lips tight against the backflow. They wouldn't be asking for more. I looked down. Bobo had wolfed all the salt-and-vinegars, and was licking the ripped bag. Bunky got too close and took a giant paw thump on the head for it. The water bowl was three-quarters empty.

"What're you gonna do, sit there and jerk that bottle neck all night?" Terry said.

I filled his glass and Augie's. They laughed, clinked glasses, and turned away. No more use for me. The bartender stood there. "Get me another Coke," I said.

As soon as the bartender turned, I did it. I took the bottle down and dumped it, more than half the bottle of crystal clear, smooth as ice Stolichnaya Russian vodka, into Bobo's bowl. Seasoned brass-balled drinker that he was, champion stud mauler, Bobo didn't even blink as he lapped it dry. When he was finished, he looked up longingly at me. Pathetically, desperately, he kept on licking, that fat brown tongue sweeping over his glistening teeth, over his bristly whiskers, over his blunt stupid snout again and again as if he had peanut butter smeared all over him. He smelled mostly of vinegar.

I thought it was funny. Then I looked into his innocent, ignorant black eyes, and I was pricked with pity for him.

"Hey, Augie," I said, "your dog's really thirsty, give him a drink quick."

"Ya, well, so am I. You give me one."

"Can't," I said, holding up the bottle. "You boys killed it."

Terry and Augie shrieked and head-butted each other, as if they'd just reached the top of Everest. Bobo kept licking, whimpering now.

I gave Bobo my Coke, told the bartender to fill the water bucket. Bobo drank the Coke, and the bucket, and another bucket.

"It's time, goddamnit," Terry said.

They all got up and toddled toward the back, Augie yanking on Bobo's chain. Bobo followed, in line, took a few sideways steps, banged off the corner of the bar, got back in line, and went out to meet the Doberman.

I wasn't going to go. I was above that. I felt sorry for Bobo. Bobo wasn't my concern. Screw Bobo. I was going to leave. I sat on my stool, drank my Coke to the sounds of the growling and snarling and the dogs. I found myself leaning in that direction anyway, hanging on every bit of it, piecing it together the way kids must have in the radio days. I got lost in it.

"Here, kid. They're gone now. You got nothing ta prove. It's on me."

The bartender leaned in to me, slid a hopping popping cold pint of draft under my nose. He stood back smirking and watched me. The bubbles jumped up at me, tickling my nose. I did not pull my nose away. It smelled delicious. Hoppy. It was Bass ale. Nothing else smells like that. But Bass doesn't have those bubbles. It was Bass and Rolling Rock together. I stuck my nose practically into the drink, got the tiniest bit of foam on the tip of my pointer nose.

I heard a bark, huge, like a gong. Dogs don't bark when they fight. It was Bobo. I pushed the glass over, watched it spread out across the bar before I walked back to the bullring.

Bobo wasn't fighting. He stood, listing, in the middle while the Doberman ran hysterical circles around him, looking for an opening. Bobo simply rotated ponderously, like a circus elephant on a tiny platform. The Doberman got around back, took a nip of Bobo's leg. Did it again. Did it again. The locals were popping blood vessels screaming at Bobo. The Jamaicans folded their arms. One of them smiled.

"Pussy," Terry screamed at Bobo. "Fight, faggot dog. I'll kick your ass myself."

Augie wasn't a lot of help from his champion's corner. "Bo! Bobo. Bobo Bobo. Fuckin' Bobo." His voice cracked when the Doberman opened a gash on Bobo's hip.

One step slow, ten degrees off center, Bobo couldn't seem to pull it together. It got pathetic, watching the smallish, lean and angry dog kicking hell out of the big bull. One more lunge, the Doberman snagged Bobo's ear. He pulled and pulled, the way a normal dog will play tug of war with a stick. He dug in deep with his paws, and yanked convulsively, pulling Bobo's hide like a sweater over his head. Bobo made not a sound as he held his ground, head pointed down, and blood poured over his eyes.

I was more ashamed than I had ever been in my whole shame-infested life. My throat felt as if there was a whole walnut stuck in it. I took three quick steps toward the fray, as if I could *help* now.

Like a cornerback out of nowhere, Terry banged into me, chest to chest.

"Don't you never, *never* break up a dogfight, you got that? Don't you *never* even think about it. The loser is *supposed* to lose, that's how we get rid of the weaklings. And not that I fuckin' care, but you get in between there, and they'll fuckin' eat your ass, understand? And believe this, boy, I *won't put my hand in there f'you.*"

Somehow, Terry made me feel like I was in

danger. I took a step back. Even though I could still hear the sickening fight, it was now easier to take, looking into Terry's mug instead of Bobo's. The crowd noise had remained loud, but had switched to a filthy choir of vile attacks on Bobo. I looked at the other faces, saw even more hate than usual. I remembered Terry's speech on the meaning of dogs, realized that they all believed it. I hoped the dog would die in the fight, for his own sake.

"Faggot, Bobo, go for his *dick*, why dontcha."

"Hope he bones ya up the ass when he's done, Bo."

"Shoulda let little Bunky the rat terrier fight instead."

Terry half turned away from me, to make his point while pointing at the fight as if it was a lesson on a blackboard rather than one animal killing another. "He goddamn *deserves* what's happenin' to him. I hope it gets—"

Terry stopped, as did everyone else, when they saw it. All experienced sports fans here, they all recognized it when the Doberman made a mistake. Bobo was cut and oozing from four different spots, but it was all pretty superficial—except for the dangling ear. The Doberman had him beat on passion, but not on sheer bulk and muscle. He didn't understand that. So he thought it was time to go for the kill.

The Doberman released his grip on Bobo's head, pulled back, and dove for the belly. He reached it, but not in time to clamp his jaws shut. Seeing the smaller animal stretched out under him, Bobo acted out of dumb, vicious animal instinct. He dropped, his huge head sinking hard, with all his weight behind it, and flattened his opponent beneath him. In a heartbeat his great mouth opened, then slammed closed, across the Doberman's back. The sound of all those vertebrae smashing was like a car rolling onto a gravel driveway.

Just like that, Bobo became General Schwarzkopf returning from Desert Storm. With the cheering, I couldn't hear what Terry was yelling in my face from only three feet away. The Jamaicans filed out slowly but purposefully, the front man holding up an envelope fat with money, then tossing it on the ground. They left their corpse. A special exception to the remove-your-victim rule, since Bobo was still lying across the poor sonofabitch.

For his part, Bobo looked around numbly at the celebration, turning his brainless head in all directions, looking at everyone and appreciating nothing. Bunky ran and ran little rings around himself, mental, yipping.

The mob moved inside. I lingered, staring as blankly at Bobo as he did at me. There was a whistle from inside. Slowly, painfully, the big monster rose and padded into the bar. A minute later I followed him.

Augie was cleaning up the mess on his fighter's legs and head, blotting with a peroxide-soaked dish towel from the kitchen. Within a minute I heard ten different people say how "we" had kicked the Jamaicans' asses. Bobo pulled away from Augie and collapsed on the floor in front of his water bowl. Augie let him, and turned back to the bar to celebrate even though Bobo was still bleeding.

Terry stared for a minute as Bobo seemed to cough, or spasm, then rest his head on the floor, then spasm again, then close his eyes.

He came over and put his arm around me. I threw it off. He squeezed the back of my neck.

"C'mere, I'll walk ya out," he said.

"I guess I'm leaving," I answered.

Outside, Terry gave me a little shove, a boost out the door.

"Pretty strange, huh? Bobo's performance?"

"Ya," I said, getting ready to run.

"So, you said you might know a dog. Remember? That can beat Bo?"

"I might," I said.

"Good. Good, that's good. We'll pencil you in then. Now that this is outta the way, we're lookin' for some new meat. You're *in*," he said menacingly.

"Well, okay, but y'know, the thing is, I'm not exactly sure I can get—"

"Y'ever noticed, Mick, how when Bobo drinks too much, when he's wasted, that he hiccups? He hiccups a lot, it's the damnedest thing." Terry looked up in the air and stroked his chin quizzically as he said it.

"I never noticed that," I said in a shaky voice.

"Ya, it's a true fact. Ever wonder what Augie might do, if he caught someone screwing around with his dog? Ever wonder about that? I wonder about it sometimes. Augie's pretty fried right now, so he don't see much of nothin', but if he ever somehow did find out about something like that, if something like that ever did actually did happen . . . ?"

I didn't answer. I didn't figure I was supposed to.

He got lighter and more casual about it, the closer he got to the nub.

"And I won't stick my hand in any damn

dogfight for you. Did I tell you that already? I think I did, I told you that. Did I?"

I nodded. I swallowed. It was so hot, even outside. I felt the beads bubbling down my neck. I could see steam on the few windows of the Bloody.

"Good, I'm glad I told you that. Because I meant it. Now, what you do is, you run along, and you get that dog, and you train his ass off. We're scheduling you now. You're a priority."

He patted my cheek and faded back into the bar. I wobbled home.

Priority

The days got long, having to be up so early, scrubbing shit out of the O'Asis first thing, only to then have nothing to do the rest of the day. Most times I went back to bed when I got home. And I slept, even though I wasn't really tired. Sully had a summer job, "doin' absolutely nothin'" at the State House because his father was one of those guys who get that stuff. But he had a place to go at least. Me, I was wading through my first summer without either Little League or beer, and I was stupefied at what little there was around me. Still, I had my *focus*.

I rousted Sully out of bed as soon as I got back from work.

"C'mon, Sul, I want you to go with me."

He rolled over, away from me. I shook him harder.

"Get outta here, Mick, lemme sleep. I gotta be to work by eleven. Or eleven thirty."

"Bang in sick," I said.

He sat up and scowled at me. "Listen, this gig lasts ten weeks. They only allow me six official paid sick days and a couple more unofficial mental health days. I can't go squandering 'em."

"Fine, I'll just have to do it alone," I said—moaned, really—as I walked extra slowly away. He was always a sucker for that stuff.

"What? What is it you're gonna have to do alone?" he asked, stopping me in the doorway.

"Dog shopping."

He threw himself back on the bed and pulled his pillow around his ears. "Dogs, dogs, Jesus, please, not the dog business again, Mick. I wish you'd just forget about this dog business, man, it's no damn good. I can smell this one a mile away, and this whole dog thing, it stinks." From his lying-down position, he pointed at me menacingly. "It's gonna be your biggest fall yet."

I waited him out. I was way beyond really listening. "I gotta get a dog."

"Besides, my old man says you can't keep one anyway."

"I don't plan to keep it long. It won't be a pet. I mean, it *can't* be a pet. I'm gonna keep it at work. There's a lot, out behind the O'Asis, where I can chain him."

"Outside?"

"Ya, outside. The kind of dog I'm lookin' for isn't the kind that's gonna care whether he lives inside or out. In fact, the kind I'm lookin' for probably won't know the difference."

"It stinks."

"Bang in sick."

"No."

"Fine, you just go ahead and quit on me too. We all know I have, like, a million friends anyway, right, so it's not really a big deal. And family, let's not forget family. I have other brothers besides you, so, really, Sul, don't give it another thought." I had to say it all like a joke, but he knew I was being true.

"Asshole," he said, rolling out of bed and yanking up his pants.

As we walked up the driveway to the Animal Rescue League entrance, I thought of Mickey the dog, dumped right there on the curb like a sack of garbage. Mickey wasn't mean enough. Or big enough, or deranged enough. I needed a monstrous, ferocious, toothy, and muscular criminal of a heartless beast.

"We'd like to see your death row dogs, please," Sully said as we stood at the front desk.

The woman in the park ranger–type uniform was not amused.

"You wish to adopt one of our abandoned animals?" she asked sternly.

"Yes, I would," I cut in before Sully could empty his already opened mouth.

We followed the ranger woman down a long white hospital-like corridor. Sully continued to work on me.

"You won't do this. It ain't in you, Mick. It ain't you. You don't have the heart for this, you have too *much* heart for this."

I didn't answer, just plowed on until we got to the room with the orphans.

"Take your time, look them all over carefully," the woman said, then left us alone.

Sully and I walked side by side along the cages. Three tiers high and twenty doors long, it was like a housing project for dogs, or a prison. All cages were the same size, regardless of the dog inside, so the biggest ones were just dopily curled on the floor while the little ones jumped up and yipped as we passed.

Every single dog was a puzzle. Beagle-collie-setter. Shepherd-Doberman-Labrador. Scotty-mastiff-bassett-chow.

"Bet Father's Day is a pretty confusing time for these poor slobs," Sully cracked, scratching a mutt's nose with the two fingers he could squeeze through the mesh.

I didn't bother trying to touch any of them. I scanned. Too small, too small, too small, too skinny, jaws too narrow.

"Take this one, Mick," Sully called, still in crouching position in front of the most anemic-looking creature in the place. Sully was in love already.

"We're here on business, Sul," I said, continuing my search.

"I think maybe this little guy'll change your mind, though," he said, giggling as the dog squeezed his tongue through the bars to lick his face.

"I don't want my mind changed," I said.

A mostly Great Dane with the sad, stupid face of a St. Bernard leaped at me as I passed. Twice he rammed his head into the cage door, barking. I took note, and moved on. A boxer-bulldog glared at me, beautiful posture, big chest, crooked brown teeth. Not enough. I neared the end of the line, reaching what seemed to be the pit bull ghetto. Four dogs in a row that all had that unmistakable square, ignorant, sneering face. Like a team, they snarled one long threatening rumble as I neared.

"I'll give you all four of those monsters for the price of one," the ranger's voice said from behind me. "More and more of those coming in every week. Our city's pit bull population has been exploding, and nobody seems to have the strength to keep them from fornicating at will."

I stared in petrified awe at the shimmering menace in each of those cages. They growled so intensely, with such obvious hate, that they trembled. They certainly had some of the qualities I was looking for. They would be holy terrors, without question. But not one of them was *the* dog. The one that could overwhelm the whole world of other dogs. I could picture Bobo sitting down on top of one of those and, his own body hacked up again, swallowing big chunks out of the little bastard.

I walked back the other way again. When I reached the Dane, he was taking a gargantuan dump. He watched me as he did, growling, excreting, looking at my face. Like he was saying, "This one's for you, pal." Then he was finished and, the feces way too big to fall through the grate floor, he threw himself down on it. He stood again, looked at it. Took a bite. Looked at me. Went to the cage door and started chewing on the metal so hard that it was only a matter of time before he did get out.

"I want him," I said.

"You don't want *him*," she said.

"Yes I do."

"That one's not right, if you ask me," she said.

"Then I won't ask you. That is exactly the dog I want. Wrap him up."

The woman let out an angry low growl of her own as she went to get a leash. "Ah, I see," she said with disgust, "another one of *them*."

We waited for the shots, the tags, the brief exams. I paid my thirty-five dollars and took possession of my beast.

It all took twice as long as it should have, because Sully bought the anemic dog.

"Where are you gonna keep him?" I asked nervously as my dog alternately jerked me down the street and stopped to turn on me.

"I'll keep him at home," Sully said, all blissed

out as he carried and nuzzled his measly little half-hairless. "My dad said *you* couldn't have a dog. There's no way he won't love Bugs."

"Bugs? You named him already?" I shouldn't have been surprised. The dog actually did look like a tiny Bugs Bunny, tan, white face, satellite-dish ears.

"That's right. Bugs. What are you gonna call yours?"

"Hmmm . . ." I said, looking at my star athlete from behind. His ass showed prominently because he had a curled tail like a husky. I smiled. "I'm gonna call him . . ." And the smile left me. "Nothing."

"Nothing?"

I shook my head. "He's not gonna need a name. He's not that kind of dog."

"Pretty weird, Mick," Sully said. "But he's your dog. Listen, I'm going home now. Can't wait to show Bugs to my mother. You're not bringing Nothing to the house, are ya?"

"Nah, I'm gonna bring him ta meet my dad," I said as sarcastically as I could. Sully didn't even notice, as he skipped off with his new love.

My father was the only conscious person in the O'Asis when Nothing and I walked in. Two guys dozed at the bar, the little oscillating fan waving between them, not even disturbing their greasy mats of hair. My mother was out grocery shopping for the bar.

". . . and I figure he can watch that back door, so nobody tries to break in," I said.

My father seemed half asleep himself, one eye on the overhead TV, where ESPN was running a repeat of a hockey game to cool off the summer sweats.

"That's fine, Mick," he said. "It'll be a good deterrent. He looks mean as shit. That's good. We could use a presence like that." He winced at something that happened in the hockey game. "Jeez, so could the Bruins."

I wrestled the dog out the back door. We had already worked up a strange, unfriendly truce. He kept growling at me, kept leering at me, tossed me side to side, and ignored most of what I said, but he never tried to bite me to shreds. Which we both knew he could have done whenever he wanted to.

"But Mick," Dad said, "I don't want to know about him. You take care of all his needs, don't let him stink, and keep him quiet. And if anyone ever does try to get in here, he *better* chew the bastard's ass off."

I stuffed the dog out the door, followed him, and slammed it behind us. Immediately, Nothing broke away from me, went to a corner, and flopped in the sun. I looked around. This time of day, the back alley—a slab of asphalt surrounded by a six-foot wooden fence—was totally washed in the straight-up sun. There was no escape. I went back inside, filled a mop bucket with water and ice.

"Anybody gonna eat this?" I asked, pointing to the two half-eaten platters on the bar. One was a hamburger plate, fries, runny coleslaw, and the other was a tuna boat, fries, runny coleslaw. Nobody answered me, so I scooped it all onto one plate and brought it out to Nothing.

He nearly knocked me over when I set the plate down, and I felt a small swell of evil pride as I watched him slobber.

"See ya tomorrow, killer," I said, boldly patting his hip.

He growled, nasty, as I slipped away.

The routine became, I opened the back door, Nothing charged me, I threw a foot-long hot dog across the lot, he chased it, and I came out with the full plate of scraps. Out of the refrigerator I was allowed to take whatever was left over from the previous day's special. Knockwurst; rubbery sirloin tips; green beef stew; chopped, reconstructed turkey breast slices. Then I did my work. Then I went back out to find a much calmer Nothing. While he sat, I cleaned up his place too. Dung, mostly, but often as not I'd also come across pieces of skinny cats or fat-ass rats that were dumb enough to wander in during the night. The ferocious destruction he laid on those animals gave me hope. And still, it was less disgusting to clean up outside the O'Asis than in it.

Following the cleanup, I'd take Nothing for his run. He galloped like a Clydesdale, thundering after anything that moved, menace on his tiny little mind. He pulled me down sometimes, didn't stop, didn't slow down, even with all my weight hanging on the leash until I'd scrambled back to my feet. I watched him, over a short time, fill out impressively. His chest and shoulders and even his head seemed broader and more solid than when I first saw him. And even if he was getting a potbelly from all the fatty raw meat, he could still chug like a train.

We'd return, me sweating, him panting, and he gave me no trouble about going back into the alley. Then, before leaving, I'd skim some of the food I was *not* supposed to take—today's special, which wasn't much better than the old stuff—and I'd feed him again.

"He's ready," I told Sully after I'd had Nothing for two weeks. I'd just come in, breathless from my morning at the O'Asis, and Sully was dressing for work.

"My dad changed his mind," Sully said glumly. "He said Bugs smells, and he can't live in the house."

"Jeez, I'm sorry, Sul," I said, but I was having a hard time appreciating the problem. I had the *Big Thing* on my mind.

"He said he'd build Bugs a . . ." Sully sort of gasped when he said it, ". . . *dog*house." He scooped Bugs up where he was lying on the bed, and he hugged him.

"Oh," I said. "Well, at least you get to keep him."

"Ya, I suppose," he said.

"So, anyway, he's ready. Sul, Nothing's ready. Tonight's the night. It pissed rain on him yesterday, and it's gonna be hellish hot today, and he's gonna be meeeean. . . ."

"Congratulations," he said lifelessly.

"You gonna come with me?"

He threw me a look, then walked right past me. I grabbed his shoulder to ask him again.

Bugs let out a screamy little arf, and bit my hand with those sharp teeth.

"Ow! Jesus, Sul, can't you control him?"

"No. Neither one of us wants to discuss this

subject. You go wherever you want tonight, leave us out of it."

"I know what you think, Sul, and actually, I agree in a way. But this is *it* for me. This is the thing, the one and final *thing* that I just have to take care of. Then it'll be no more. I gotta get this done. I gotta *beat* him, Sul, for good."

Sully shook his head at me, stroked Bugs. I seemed to have made him very sad. "I don't know, Mick. Definitely, there's something out there that's eatin' you up alive, and I guess you gotta get it before it gets you . . . but I don't think messin' with Terry is gonna fix you up."

I reached out and tried to stroke the dog. He snapped at me again.

"Yes it is, Sul," I said. It was the first time I had come out with it, to anyone. It was the first time I had said it to myself. "Beating Terry, beating him into the ground, is the only way. The only single thing I'm absolutely sure of at this point is that I know I cannot exist knowing that he exists at the same time. He won't go away, understand? Somehow, he has a hold of me, and he's beating me, even right now."

Sully took a long pause and a step back. "Mick, let me try this one time. You're brainblown. Your brother has got you so screwed up, you have no perspective. You're acting exactly the way he wants you to act. You're losing a mind game to a guy who has no mind whatso-ever."

He was right! There it was. That instant, Sully showed it to me, what he could see, and probably everyone else could see but me. How stupid I looked because I was getting so blind with hate. I could see it all, just like that.

Then it was gone again, just like that.

I could kill Terry, kill him, that evil sonofa-bitch.

"After tonight, Sul. It'll be all fixed, after tonight. It'll be all better, and I won't have any more problem."

I went to the phone to make my date, while Sully walked down the stairs shaking his head and squeezing his dog.

Bloody Sundays was buzzing when Nothing and I came through the front door. A lot of mouths dropped open at the sight of the animal I could barely restrain on the choke chain. Everybody offered to buy me a drink, but I didn't even turn my head as I went through to the ring. Nothing and I took up our spot at the far corner and waited. He didn't know what was going on, and stared casually in all directions. I was so scared, the dog growled at me for jerking him so much with my shaking grip on his collar.

The spectators began filing in, lining the walls, all loaded and thrilled to be so close to the danger. I felt Nothing tense at the unfamiliar crowd. When we were at capacity, things quieted. They seemed to sense that Bobo the champion had arrived.

But first, my brother walked through the door. He came right over, sized up the dog, and nodded.

"That's a lotta meat ya got there, Mick. Good build, powerful."

I didn't say anything, just tried to stare coldly ahead like I'd seen the Jamaicans do. I was even more nervous with Terry than I'd ever been before. Thinking about what Sully said, I got defensive, lost any confidence I might have had. What's he doing to me now? I thought. What's his angle? What does he want me to say to that? I won't.

He kept smiling that smile. He started mixing conversation about the dog with conversation about me. "Has he had a lot of fights? How they treating ya there at Sullivans', huh, Mick? What're ya feedin' him? What're they feedin' you? What breeds? How's the spic chic, that workin' out okay? Animal Rescue League? Heard ya lost your boyfriend, too bad, but I heard ya had his mother, so good f'you. What I really wanna know is, did ya train him y'self, bro?"

I managed to nod.

Somehow his smile grew even wider. "Gooood," he said. "I was hopin' ya did." And as he spoke, he walked backward, bowing, all the way to the opposite side of the ring. "I'll say hi ta Ma for ya," he said, waving.

The champion emerged. Bobo and Augie strutted through the door reeking of confidence, Bunky hopping and yapping circles around them. The home crowd cheered, and they took their position beside Terry, opposite us.

At the sight of Nothing, Bobo started jumping, lunging, pulling so that it took both Terry and Augie to hold him. I had no such problem. First, Nothing didn't move. Then, I felt him leaning backward, into me. I nudged him, pushed his weight off me toward the center of the ring. Bobo growled like a volcano. Nothing backed into me again, hard.

"Goddamnit," I said under my breath, pushing him again. "Don't do this to me."

He pushed even harder, backing me up. The murmur started. By the time Nothing, with all his cowardly bulk, slammed me into the fence, people were laughing openly at me.

"Goddamn you," I shouted, snapping the leash off the collar and slapping the dog's behind. "Get in there."

Augie was first angry, then confused. Since there was no fight, he didn't know what to do. Bobo felt no such confusion. He wanted a piece of Nothing, and who could blame him? Augie shrugged, held the leash.

Terry reached across Augie and released the leash clip.

Bobo came barreling toward us, low growls rolling up out of him as he pounded his way. I froze against the fence, staring straight into his murderous mouth.

That was when Nothing finally displayed his strength. He turned, and with one powerful stroke leaped up onto the fence. He soared straight over my head, catching the top of the fence with his front legs. I hit the ground when Bobo came sailing after him, crashing into the fence, falling, jumping again. Nothing scrambled, scrambled, his back legs kicking maniacally to push him up. The crowd was in hysterics as he finally toppled over, pulling his foot out of Bobo's mouth as he did. He howled off down the street, like a siren fading away.

I kept my head down as I walked the gauntlet back through the ring, and then through the

Bloody. None of the ridicule was words, none of it mattered, except when I heard Terry, clear and crisp and hard by my ear.

"No doubt about it, you're the guy that trained that dog. But don't worry about it, boy. Don't worry. Nothin' ta be *ashamed* of. Nothin' at all. Get another dog. Just get another dog. Come back. We'll be here. You'll come back. Get another dog. We'll be here. . . ." And on and on he went, talking at me through the bar, and after I'd left the bar, and as I slept off and on that night.

A Little Bit Free

As I headed out to work in the morning I passed the doghouse Sully's father had built for Bugs. I'd walked right by it the night before, but in the light it was amazing. Real asphalt shingles for the roof, three colors of paint, a swinging door to keep out the cold, and shuttered windows. I walked across the lawn to it, crouched, and opened the shutters.

"Bar-ar-ar-ar-ar!" Bugs shocked me with his annoying angry yap. I heard his teeth clack together like silverware as he tried repeatedly to bite me, and I fell back on the grass.

"Should have brought *you*," I said as I brushed myself off and left him still barking.

For the last time I went out back of the O'Asis and cleaned up after my big brute of a dog. I could still hear them laughing in my ears. Then I trudged through my usual chores, and when I was done, absentmindedly went to the refrigerator for food.

"Duh," I said to myself, and put the plastic bag full of stew beef back. Then I thought about it and took it out again.

I rode the bus back toward the house, but continued on one extra stop. There I got off, walked a little way, and stood for a bit in front of Evelyn's house. After giving myself a few minutes to think it over one more time, I crept around the side.

The great creature didn't get up when he saw me. Initially he didn't even raise his head. I took a few tentative steps into the yard, reached into the bag, and pulled out some chunks of meat. I tossed them toward where the dog lay half in, half out of his house. He licked them up off the ground, chewed once, swallowed, then looked at me again. I threw a few more. With each toss, I took a couple steps further into the yard until the bag was empty and I was almost within reach of his chain.

"I'll be back tomorrow," I said, and slipped out before he finished the last of it.

I did come back tomorrow. And the next day. The beef was his favorite, but he was also happy to have the turkey, sausages, ham, and even the bogus cod croquettes I was almost afraid to give him. I began to look forward to feeding him, and he seemed to be glad to see me. I hurried through my work every day so I could get there.

He was the one. I knew all along he was the one. I would take it slowly, bring him along. There was no rush anyway; I felt no urgency, no panic, because it was so obvious that this was the one and that it was all going to come to an end soon enough.

My days then, sweaty, long, and secretive still, took on an odd, unexpected calmness. I had some kind of rhythm for the first time since school, Toy, and all that ended. I did my work, I visited the dog, and then I did other stuff. There was other stuff to do, now that I felt the Big One was coming along.

Slowly I gained some strength and some confidence, as if I were dipping into Baba's steroids. The feeling came back in my fingers and toes, the numbness I'd been carrying around for weeks without noticing faded. And feelings came back elsewhere. It was very hot and humid.

Or maybe it was Toy being gone that brought back those feelings.

I checked to see that the motorcycle wasn't parked outside, then I started throwing rocks. Ping, ping. Bang, I hit her window every time. Finally she came to the window, looked down and saw me, covered her eyes with her hand, and shook her head. Then she disappeared.

I was still out on the sidewalk looking up, uncertain what she was going to do, when she opened the front door.

"Come on, get in off my sidewalk," she said, waving me in hurriedly.

My shockability had been pretty well eroded by this time, but when I followed Felina upstairs into the apartment, I was shocked. First was her smell. As I walked along behind her, she left me in a wake, a vapor trail of unwashed human smell. A person's got to bathe regularly in steamy heat like this, and she clearly had not. To make it worse, every door and window in the place had been sealed shut and there wasn't a fan or an air conditioner in sight.

The house was a wreck. Dirty clothes lined the floors and I stepped on a loaf of bread on the way to the kitchen. There I stood in the doorway as Felina approached the stove and stared at it as if she were looking under the hood of a hopelessly broken-down car. She picked up the tea kettle, shook it to feel its contents, smiled, and lit the burner.

"Ah, I'm sorry I haven't called," I said as I looked around the kitchen, at the sink mounded with dirty dishes, at the table mounded with possibly clean laundry.

She put her hand over her mouth and laughed. "That's all right," she said, and patted my cheek as she passed on her way to the living room. "You're sweet."

The living room was no better. She plopped herself down on the couch after sweeping a white takeout carton and an empty wine bottle onto the floor. The TV was already on. She waved me over, and I sat reluctantly next to her.

Barney the dinosaur was on the TV. She stared at it, but I could tell she wasn't really looking.

"You want me to change that?" I asked.

"If you want to," she said, shrugging. "It doesn't much matter. I just keep it on for, you know, the sound of it. And the moving. It's always on."

The kettle screamed in the kitchen. I watched Felina some more, but there was no reaction to this either. I pointed toward the kitchen with my thumb.

"You want me to get that?" I asked.

She stood without answering, went out, and turned it off. She returned with no tea and sank back into the couch. Barney sang a song, his gang of kids sang the song. Felina sang the song too.

> *"If all the raindrops*
> *were lemondrops and gumdrops*
> *oh what a rain that would be*
> *standing outside with my mouth open*
> *   wide."*

She opened her mouth and let her tongue hang out like the rest of the kids, still singing,

> *"Ah, ah-ah-ah*
> *ah-ah-ah*
> *ah-ah-ah . . . "*

When the song was over, Felina clapped for herself and started laughing. "Where did I learn *that*?"

Then she went blank again.

"Hey, I know," I said after waiting in vain for her to say anything that made sense to me. "Why don't we go out to breakfast? Ya, how 'bout to the diner? They have a corned beef hash over there, with an egg on top, and hash browns with crunchy onions, and a really thick chocolate milk . . . Pat's Diner, that's it. On me, okay, you could hop in the shower. . . ." I hopped up and gestured toward the door, as if it had already been decided. I was anxious to get out.

She looked up and smiled at me sadly. "I don't go out. You know that. Didn't I tell you that? I don't go out."

"Ever?" I asked.

She shrugged. "It's not . . . okay. It's not okay, that I go out."

It made me angry, both the situation and the fact that she was so calm about it. My hands balled into nervous fists, until I thought about Carlo and all his bulk and darkness. My fists uncurled.

"Well, what would happen if you just went out? Just for a little while?"

Felina shook her head no. She turned back to the TV, turned off the subject.

"Do you miss him?" she asked quietly.

I paused, as if I had to think about who she meant, even though I didn't.

"You do miss him," she said. "I'll *bet* you do. I miss him too. Do you miss him the way *I* miss him?" There was so much sticky hot suggestion in the way she drawled out that *I*, that it made me squirm. "I bet you do. I bet you do miss him that way. It certainly is sad," she whispered, her voice getting lower and lower so that I had to strain harder and closer to hear her.

I wanted to change the subject—not change it so much maybe as slant it differently. "You know where he is?" I asked, backing toward the door.

"You know better than that," she said. She reached her hand into the pocket of her bath-robe, took something out, and popped it into her mouth. In the same motion she untied the sash. She seemed almost unaware of me then.

"Okay, so then, maybe another time," I said. I turned the doorknob behind my back.

Felina snapped her head in my direction. She stood up, a little panicky. The robe hung open, but I tried not to notice. "Wait," she said, and put her hand on the door. "I can do it. What the hell, right? Sit. You sit for a minute."

She practically threw me onto the couch, then disappeared down the hall. I sat with Barney for an uneasy few minutes until she reappeared.

She had ignored my advice about showering, but she had made an effort. The great mass of her hair was still a chaotic and snarled and oily mess, but she had wrestled it into a giant meatloaf of an uncombed ponytail. She wore stonewashed shorts and a neon peach T-shirt that had a picture of a sailboat and a seagull and HAMPTON BEACH, NEW HAMPSHIRE—SUMMER BETTER THAN OTHERS printed in raised rubbery lettering across the chest. Except for being unclean and sleepy, she looked pretty beautiful. She wore a lot of bitter perfume. I was happy to be with her.

We didn't talk at all. Felina smiled a lot as we walked the five blocks. She stared almost exclusively up at the sky, or out the window by our booth. She ordered everything I had mentioned—the hash, the egg, the chocolate milk—exactly the same way I had said it. As if it were a command. I ordered the same. People stared at us and the waitress seemed to wince whenever she came near, but I had a fine time, and the smile never left Felina's face. Even when she briefly nodded off.

During the walk home, she would periodically close her eyes and bare her greenish face to the now blistering noon sun. I got a panic attack as we came nearer to her street, but it all washed away when we turned the corner and there was still no motorcycle. I would have gone all the way to the house with her anyway, but I was sure glad it didn't come to that.

Felina didn't even turn to look at me, lost and happy as she seemed to be, as I left her walking up her stairs. But that was okay.

Duran

"What are you doing back there?" Evelyn called out her window, nearly giving me a stroke. I was in her backyard and her dog was eating boneless spareribs out of my hand.

I'd been at it for two weeks, feeding him, then patting him, finally talking to him. That was probably what gave me away, the talking.

"He *likes* you?" she said, standing amazed and barefoot on her back porch. "He doesn't like *anybody*."

"He likes me," Ruben said, following his sister out through the screen door.

"He *hates* you," she cracked.

"That's a freakin' lie," Ruben said, brushing past her to march down the stairs. When he reached the third step, the dog started snarling. Ruben walked backward up onto the porch again.

"Well, I ain't got no shoes on, so I can't go into the yard right now, but I'll show you all later. Freakin' dog loves my ass."

"He hates you because you neglect him," Evelyn said matter-of-factly.

I patted the dog's wide muscular head as he easily lapped up the last of the food. As he chewed, the muscles flexed on either side of the part that ran down the middle of his skull. I could fit both hands flat across that magnificent dome of his and feel his bite while he ate. And he let me.

"Atsa boy, boy," I said, but he paid no attention.

"His name's Duran," Ruben said, "and he ain't no boy."

He was right about that, for sure. But that's what I had been calling the dog all along, boy. Duran, though, was great. It fit the second I heard it. "Du-ran," I repeated, and patted him, scratched the sides of his face, and looked into his beady one-black-one-green eyes.

"You the loneliest sombitch I ever seen,"

Ruben laughed as he headed back into the house.

"Ya?" Evelyn called to him. "Bet he doesn't have one of those blow-up dolls in his room . . ."

"Shut up, Juana," he yelled. "That's just a freakin' joke. *Christo*, ain't like I *do* nothin' wid it."

Ruben went up to put on his shoes and not do anything with his doll. Evelyn stood and watched me with the dog. He leaned into me, responding, rubbing his eyes across my chest. "You're a pair," she said, with some admiration.

"We are," I answered, then I looked up. "You heard anything, from him?"

"*Nada*," she said flatly.

"Me neither. I talked to his mother though."

Evelyn shook her head in a scolding way, clicked her tongue at me.

"Ya, well, she doesn't know where he is either," I said. "I guess it's for good this time."

She just shrugged. Ruben came bounding back out onto the porch. Duran growled, and I calmed him.

"I want to take him for a walk," I said, hopping up, thinking this was a bright idea for a beautiful worthless summer day.

They both gasped, as if I said I wanted to throw open a nuclear reactor. "A walk?" Ruben said. "Where you gonna walk him? I take him down the freakin' park once a night, after everybody else goes home, and he drags my ass all over the place. I can only just barely shove him back here in the yard, and I can only do that 'cause he knows Evelyn throws some food out here for him while we're out. You can't handle him, man, no way."

He was serious, with his intense frown. He wasn't just trying to run me down and un-man me like usual. He didn't think what I wanted to do was possible. Then a dopey, distant smile opened his face up.

"He *is* fun, though," Ruben said warmly. "You know he could *kill* my ass anytime he wants to, but he don't. He just throws me around like I'm a freakin' toy. An' sometimes, when he's in a good mood, I ride him."

Evelyn looked disgusted with her brother, which was not unusual. "Ruben, you *ride* that poor animal?"

"Poor *nothin'*," he said. "Lookit 'im. Freakin' Duran's half a horse. He loves to ride, no foolin'. He goes even faster when I'm on his back than when I ain't. You know that track around the park? Four freakin' hundred meters. He carried me around four laps one night last week, and he don't wanna stop. Only reason we quit was that *I* was gettin' sore."

I could barely hide my enthusiasm. "Let's take him out, let's go, let's go now."

"No way, can't do it. One, he don't like me so good in the daytime—"

"Nobody does," Evelyn shot.

"Two, they's too much business goin' on this time a day. Other dogs, peoples, et-freakin'-cetera. Duran gets hisself a little excited. *Loco*. Starts ta killin' up stuff."

"Please?" I begged, even more excited now.

Evelyn was way suspicious of me now. "What's the big attraction, Mick? What's the big thrill here? Could it be that you got used to the protection of walking around with one big stud and now that he's gone you need another one?"

This was what made Evelyn so special, so exciting, so impossible to resist, the way she knew so much of a person's inside stuff. And this was what made Evelyn so frightening, so maddening, so *necessary* to resist, the way she knew so much about a person's inside stuff.

"Nooo," I drawled, summoning up all my debate skills. And I left before she could do any more. Ruben followed me out of the yard.

"So, where you wanna go?" he asked brightly.

This wasn't the partner I'd expected to be walking with. "No place. I think I'll just walk home."

"Okay," Ruben said, walking right along with me. He took it as an invitation. So we walked together.

"You ever consider doing something with Duran?" I asked after we'd walked a bit.

"Doin' what?"

"You know, he's a lot of dog. It's kind of a shame not to put his talents to use. You could make a lot of money—"

"Oh, he ain't *that* fast."

"No. Come on, you know what I'm talking about, Ruben. You should fight him."

"Nah, he'd beat me easy."

"Jesus. I don't mean—"

"Man, I know what you mean. You so stupid, you think other people are stupid. I ain't talkin' about what you talkin' about 'cause I don't wanna talk about it. I told you before, my dog don't fight for no money."

This was bad, but I let it drop. He'd see, eventually. We got there, home, and I stopped short at the walkway. It was as if there was a force field there, or a checkpoint with armed guards. Sully's nutty little hairless was barking like crazy from his condo, but that wasn't it. Ruben went over to play with the dog, and they hit it right off. He turned back to look at me frozen on the sidewalk. "What?" he asked.

"What? Nothing," I said. "Let's move on."

It wasn't my house. Those people inside, those nice people, were not my family. I had no business, and no right, bringing guests by. It would have occurred to me before, if I'd ever tried it before. Now that I had, it was official. Ruben did me a favor.

We just walked then, two guys with nothing to do. Past Sully's house and on through the old neighborhood. As soon as I crossed the divider, Sycamore Street, I felt it. The foreignness. Maybe it was the beating of the sun that just would not go away. The emptiness of the streets, except for the McGinnesses' eight filthy kids running madly through every yard with a sprinkler. Mrs. Healy said hello when I walked by her short stone wall, but she says hi to everybody. Except Ruben. Mrs. Gillooly looked up from where she crouched, hacking something out of her crappy little garden. She blocked the sun from her eyes with one gloved hand, squinted at us both, then went back to work without saying anything.

"I thought you was goin' home?" Ruben said to me while staring at my old neighbors.

"Well, ya," I said. "That back there was Sully's house. I stay there now. But this is, was, my neighborhood. Where I lived. Before." I did not miss a single house as I guided Ruben through the places I used to know.

"That red, white, and blue house, that was Harney. He paid me twenty bucks when I was his paperboy and I saw him beating off in his backyard at five thirty in the morning. Wasn't a bad guy. The yellow house, with the three flagpoles, that was the Canadian couple who couldn't have any kids, so they never got invited to the cookouts, so they moved out after two years. The purple house, Mr. McCrea. He died there. He was really old. Me and Sully helped him in with his groceries—we used to always hover around because he paid big dough for help with his groceries. We brought in the bundles, left them on the table, took our money, and blasted off. He died. They went in and got him a week later, the bundles still there on the table where we left them. We tried to get a peek, Sully and me, standing on the trash barrels at the back window, but Mr. McCrea was in a bag already. We watched anyway, even though it was pretty nasty.

"The white house. The German lady with the retarded son. She remained the same age for all the time she lived there. When I collected every week for her newspaper she made me stay there for a long time. She wouldn't talk to anybody but me. Because I played a game of checkers one time with the retarded kid, who also happened to be huge. She swore she was never going to die and leave her son alone. I heard her tell him that all the time, holding his catcher's mitt of a hand while he cried like a baby. And then she would turn and tell it to me, like she was insisting, and forcing it on me would make it true. She was like a hundred when her son finally died and she died a week later. It was the greatest thing I ever saw anybody do, but nobody seemed to notice around here. My father said her husband was a big-time war criminal and they deserved ten retarded kids."

I stopped talking when, for a second, I forgot who I had been talking to. Ruben's face was expressionless as he looked at me, then away at the house nearest, where a black-and-tan mutt was barking and throwing himself at the chain-link fence to try and bite Ruben. The dog's owners sat unconcerned on the porch, fanning themselves with magazines and pressing wet Coke cans to their necks.

"Those people used to be nice," I said. "They moved in just a few years ago. Tried to get a block party going the first summer. 'We don't need no yuppie damn block party crap here,' was what everybody said. So instead, the neighborhood got together and had a multifamily disgusting blowout drunko cookout that looked a lot like a block party only no one would dare to call it that. And the blue house—guinea blue is what my father always called it—is where Rourke the fireman lives. Whenever it was hot we would automatically show up on his curb and he would come out with his enormous wrench and open up the hydrant for an hour. There, that place with the big lawn, they put out a Christmas display every year, life-size lighted plastic reindeer, nativity scene, snowmen, a billion watts of colored lights, better than Edaville Railroad—"

"I freakin' *hate* this neighborhood," Ruben interrupted.

"I don't have a single bad memory of this place," I said, momentarily comfortable with the lie.

We were almost there, at my parents' house. I grabbed Ruben's arm and reversed him down the street. "It's time to go now," I said, two houses short of the one. I gestured at it. "That was it, where I grew up, that one back there. It's time to go now," I repeated firmly.

Ruben must have found it interesting, the way I walked around and around to no place. To the baseball field where I had my only, tiny moments of stardom and where, in the left field trees, I spent my first ever all-nighter with a girl even though I never touched her. To the fruit store that was now a check-cashing place but I wanted to stand inside for a few minutes anyway. To the church where I lit every single devotional candle without donating a dime. There in that gargantuan crumbling red-rugged church I could tell by the way he stared up at the ceiling murals that Ruben and I had at least a little something in common. We didn't say anything, but I could tell. We even had the same thought at the same time and dashed to the confessional. I jumped into the priest's slot in the middle of the booth, and Ruben hopped into the confessor's slot. I slid open the small screened window between us.

"Bless me, Father, for I have sinned," he said solemnly. "I really *did* do things with that freakin' blow-up doll. . . ."

The big old church rang with our laughs, which only made us laugh harder. There was nobody in there but us, and whatever ghosts we were looking at when we each stared off for long stretches, and it was thrilling.

"Who is that?" a voice boomed from behind the altar. A door slammed with it.

"Holy shit, it's God. Let's beat it," Ruben said

as we bolted. "I was a freakin' altar boy here, can you believe it?"

"So was I," I said.

Still the motion didn't stop, and we wandered. That wasn't what I had intended to do; I kept feeling like I was en route to someplace, where I would stop, but I couldn't find the place.

"Hey," he finally said, his T-shirt dampening long after mine had soaked through. "Don't you, like, own a restaurant or somethin'? Didn't I hear that?"

"Ah, well, something like that," I said. "My parents."

"So, can't we go there? You can eat for free, right? And your friends too, probably."

Maybe it was the heat and the exhaustion. Maybe it was the fact that I wanted something from Ruben and I had very little to entice him, or anybody, with. Or maybe I just felt like, goddamnit, there must be *some* benefit, *some* small perk to being who I am, stuck with who I've got. Probably, it was all those things together, because the idea sounded good. And it was lunchtime.

The six shadowy people huddled at the little tables scattered around the O'Asis didn't notice when Ruben and I walked in. The three others at the bar didn't notice either. They were all stuck there, melted into position like one of those famous bar pictures—the *Boulevard of Broken Dreams*, or the poker-playing dogs. My father, though, he noticed. He stared wide-eyed as we strolled up to *his* bar.

"Ya?" he said to me, though he looked at Ruben. As if on cue, Ruben's hair had gotten even curlier and kinkier in the heat.

"We're looking for service," I said pleasantly.

"Why?" he asked. "You never come here."

"I figure I should maybe change that," I said. "I figure this could all be mine someday, so . . . this could be my legacy."

He was not amused. "What'll you have?" he mumbled.

My mother came out of the bathroom. "I thought that was Mick I heard. How wonderful. Can I fix . . . ?" She hitched when she saw Ruben. "Oh," she said smoothly. He smiled at her.

"I'll go fix you something," she said, and went to the refrigerator.

"Drinking?" my father asked.

"Coke," I said, matching his monotone.

"Tecate Cerveza," Ruben said, requesting his favorite, obviously-not-on-the-menu beer.

My father just waited.

"Dos Equis?" Ruben chirped.

More waiting.

"Bud," Ruben said in a voice much deeper than his real one. Bud he got.

My mother brought us two plates. Roast beef sandwiches with shoelaces of gristle running all through them. French fries soaked brown from yesterday's oil. Big dry pickle spears. I ate what I could, which wasn't much. Ruben buzzed through it all, ordered a second beer, then cleaned my plate. "Thank you," he said to my father, "that was really great." I looked for signs, but he appeared not to be joking. When he got nothing but a grunt out of my old man, he flagged down my mother, who was going around cleaning off tables. She tried to ignore him, but it was a pretty small place. "Thank you very much. You are a fantastic cook." This time I was sure, but no, he looked for all the world like he meant it.

He'd melted her a bit. She stopped wiping around the elbows that remained stuck to the table. She fumbled. "Oh. My. Oh, well, thank you . . . young man." She wasn't used to compliments.

We got up to go, leaving the scene untouched, as we found it. My father slapped a piece of paper onto the bar. I picked it up. It was a bill: one roast beef plate at $3.95 and two drafts at $1.50 each. Ruben read it over my shoulder.

"And we don't take food stamps," my father said, grinning.

Ruben ignored him, embarrassed at the position he was in. "I don't got no freakin' money," he said shyly to me.

"Oh, now *there's* a goddamn surprise," said my father.

I glared at him. "Jesus Christ," I said, crumpling his little bill. "Take it out of tomorrow's pay."

"I will," he said as we walked away.

When we hit the white sidewalk, the two of us started rubbing our eyes from the shock of the sun. When they were clear, we found my brother and Augie almost on top of us, with Bobo and Bunky in tow.

We stood, they stood, nobody talked, as both Terry and Augie gave Ruben the up and down with their eyes. Terry smiled. Augie didn't.

"So, how's the lunch?" Terry asked.

"Chewy," I snapped. "Couldn't choke it down."

"Shame," Terry said. "That's a shame. You got that dog yet? Boy? Ready for a date?" I squirmed, trying to slip the subject before Ruben caught it. For once, Augie helped me out.

"Hey," Augie said, pointing at Ruben. "Hey."

Nobody had any idea what Augie was getting at, but Ruben didn't like it anyhow. "Hey," he said back, pointing. "Hey."

"Are you the punk . . . ?" Augie continued.

Ruben couldn't stifle a laugh, right in Augie's face, at the stupidity. "Well, I'm *a* punk. I don't know if I'm *the* punk. I'm flattered, though. I like to *think* of myself as *the* punk, but there are a lot of great punks out there, as you know. . . ."

It flew right by Augie. "You the one with the dog? Sure you are. You're the one that got the dog that's supposed to be like the hottest shit there is. I been lookin' ta meet you, boy."

Already, Ruben was through playing. He would not even talk about it. "Mick, man, can we go? Let's get the hell outta here."

I nodded, but Augie pushed on. "What's the matter? I just wanna talk a little deal. This dog a yours is supposed ta be so damn great. I say Bobo kicks the livin' shit outta whatever you got."

Bobo had plunked himself down on the sidewalk in the blinding sun, with Bunky beside him standing watch. Bobo was panting hard. He had some fresh cuts around his eyes, on his snout, on his front leg. He had old cuts scarring his ears, and the hair hadn't yet grown back where he needed stitches near his hip. His eyes were glassy. Bobo was fast becoming a very old dog. He looked like an old boxer who should have quit already. Augie and Terry obviously could not see what they had, a soldier whose time had passed.

There were a whole lot of fights behind that animal, and very few left in front of him. A fight with Duran would certainly be his last.

"My dog don't fight," Ruben said finally.

"Oh he don't, do he?" Augie mocked. "Do he lick dick?"

Terry and Augie had a big laugh over that one, then Augie said to Ruben, "Hey, watch this. Wanna see what my other dog can do? He's the smart one. Name's Bunker Hill. Bunky," he called, and the smug little Boston terrier strutted over.

"You don't want to see this," I said, and nudged Ruben to move on. He just held up a hand to me, determined not to look away.

"Bunky," Augie asked, snapping his fingers, and the dog stood up on his hind legs. "What would you rather be, Bunky, Rican or dead? Rican or dead, Bunky, Rican or dead?" he repeated. Like he was shot, the little dog dropped to the pavement and lay still as a brick.

Again, Terry and Augie killed themselves laughing.

"I'm not Puerto Rican," Ruben said calmly as he brushed past them and stepped over the dogs.

"Oh, wait then," Augie called. "Bunky, up. Gook or dead, Bunky?" Bang, Bunky was down again. "Up, Bunky. Faggot or dead, Bunky?" Bang. Dead again.

I tried to leave. My brother grabbed my arm and pulled me to him. "So, that's your dog? I want it. Can you do it? Loser boy?"

I turned to him, our pointy noses together again. "I can do it," I said. "But money just isn't enough. I want more than the money. If we win, I want you gone."

He flinched.

"You understand? That's the deal. Bobo loses, and you have to clear the hell out of the house. I know you're not scheduled to move out for another ten or twelve years, but I can't wait anymore. So that's the deal. You lose, you're out, I'm in."

He actually stopped grinning for a moment. The thought of leaving the house before age thirty-five must have chilled him. But then the brainless confidence came roaring back.

"Sure," he said, "and if Bobo wins—*when* Bobo wins—I don't move out. But you do still move back in."

How he could continue to come up with the most incredibly vile ideas, even with his barely functioning brain, amazed me more than ever.

"Deal," I said, and found myself shaking as I trotted to catch up with Ruben.

"It'll be sweet," he called after me. "Just like old times."

No Matter Where It's Going

I thought about Terry while I slept. I woke up tense, dressed, rode the bus, opened up the O'Asis. Tense. After awhile I loosened up, did my rotten job, collected my pay envelope. Inside it, of course, was the bill from Ruben's lunch that I had crumpled, pressed out flat again. And the amount had been deducted from my money.

"Asshole," I said. Taking the pen off the bar, I wrote a little note of my own on the envelope. "Forgot your tip. Ruben says *gracias*." I laid the note on the bar with a dollar.

Tense.

"Hey boy," I said, walking across the yard toward Duran. I stooped to meet him, but he stretched toward me, so stooping became pretty unnecessary. He butted me, rammed me with his head, to play. Sent me four steps backward and winded me, but made me laugh too. I opened the bag and hand-fed him the fat and fatty slices of pork roast that were gray from my mother's cooking.

As I watched him eat, I thought about it. It was still early. Why not?

I unclipped his chain, and I talked to him in low easy humms. "There you go, guy," I said, stroking the side of his head, stroking the thick, taut muscles of his neck. I leaned into him and got my face close to his ear. "There we go, boy. You want to go? Just for a short one now. Just for a stretch. But easy now, okay?"

As if he understood clearly, he took his first long, direct strides. He was behaving himself fine, but he dragged me anyway. He didn't even seem to notice.

There was nobody on the street. We trotted. "Good boy, Duran. Atta boy, Duran," I chanted, praying that I was somehow controlling him. A jogger passed on the other side of the street. She looked over, mouth hanging open. He noticed her too, running on this way while looking back that way. "Never mind her, Duran, there ya go, boy," I said, and he forgot about her.

We made it to the park without incident. The only hitch was the dragging. Duran knew the way, and clearly had no need for me, so he went at his own pace. I barely kept up as his speed increased the closer he got to the park. The instant he hit the running track that ovaled the whole field, he left me behind.

The links of his chain ripped, 1-2-3-4-5-6-7-8, through my fingers. I fell, stumbling to my knees, then looked at my raw hand. Then I looked back up to where Duran was. *Loose.*

He stayed on the track. That was what he wanted. He wanted to run, and run and run, after all those hours of lying chained up in the small yard with his big long legs folded under him. And he was great at it. He had gone two hundred meters before my eye had even caught up to him, and from that spot exactly halfway across the field from me, you could not tell the difference between this animal and a racehorse.

I felt it through the ground as he thundered past me starting his second lap. He ran the second lap faster than the first, the third even faster.

I didn't want to ride him. I just wanted to watch him. So I did. Through four and five and six beautiful laps. I sat there on the grass enjoying Duran's exercise, being lightened by it, every bit as much as he must have been.

Until, a hundred meters into his seventh circuit, he bolted. Like a train jumping the tracks, Duran took one long springing dive from the running surface into the trees and bushes at the edge of the park. I jumped up and ran to where he was snarling, snapping, thrashing around, and I stopped short when I got there. He had it, in his paws and jaws at the same time like a bear catching a salmon from a rapid.

Whatever it was, there was nothing I could do for it now. I had to just let the dog finish. The way he went about it, biting and tearing and throwing pieces of whatever in all directions long after it was dead, it was like Duran had a personal thing against it. Finally, when there was nothing big enough left to bite at, Duran backed slowly out of the bushes, still sniffing and licking at the ground.

I approached him easily, holding out my hand to him. At first he didn't respond, but then he took a couple of steps my way and butted his head into my belly. I petted him, laid my hands on either side of his boxy rib cage. I felt the slight heaving, the punching of his thrilled heart. I felt it in him, then I felt it in me.

Two boys appeared, coming down the hill at the far end of the field. They had a bat and baseball gloves, and a retriever dashing in circles around them and between their legs.

"Come on, Duran," I said, giving the chain a mighty tug. He didn't budge, until I stopped pulling. Then he came along quietly as we went out the opposite way from the boys. I stopped using the chain altogether on the way home. It didn't do any good anyway. I still held it, but I didn't pull on it. Instead I just guided Duran the way cowboys do on TV when they are trying to get cattle into the corrals. I leaned into his shoulder to push him one way, I put my arm over the back of his neck to pull him the other way. I even wrapped my arms around his bullish head to steer him as if he did have horns. And he let me. It was fun and must have looked comical, but I loved it. I think Duran loved it too.

When I returned to Evelyn's to corral Duran, Toy was waiting.

"Excellent!" I said.

"Excellent? Mick, I'm here to warn you. The old man's gonna kick your ass. Don't you get it?"

Now I got it. "Why . . ? Oh . . ." I said and started pacing, wringing my hands, flashing back on the hugeness of Carlo looming over me naked in his bed.

"No, not because you tapped her," Toy said.

I ducked, actually raised my hands to my face, and gasped when Toy said it.

He shook his head in disgust and disbelief. "Of course I know, fool. But Carlo doesn't care about that. Not much, anyway. He's pissed because you messed with his *casa*. You screwed with his *control*. Carlo is a certain kind of . . . macho."

"I don't get it," I said.

"You let her out, Mick. When you took her out to breakfast? You released her. You broke the hold, get it? You went into *his* house and set free *his* possession."

Hot shit, I thought with some pride, I did all that? I stared off, thinking once more about Felina.

Toy caught me. "Forget it. She's gone. She's history. And you might be too."

"Come on," I said, laughing a little desperately, "he won't really . . ."

"Mick, I figured I ought to tell you before I leave, that's all. I'm just passing through this time but tomorrow morning I'm gone too."

"For real and for good?"

Toy pointed to the street where a motorcycle was parked. It was a different bike, smaller, older, but still a Harley-Davidson. "He bought me that for a going-away present. After my mother left, he came home with that and said, 'Happy birthday, boy. Ride it the hell on out of here.' "

"You?" I said, stunned. "I thought you two were . . ."

"He tried to mold me in his own image, but it didn't take. We've got disagreeable life-styles."

"He seemed cool," I said, only half-joking, "the couple of times we met."

Toy laughed at that. "Mick, you have a very black-and-white way of looking at things. This is good, this is bad, this is right, this is wrong, if I do A, then B will be fixed. Most stuff is more complicated than that, there's a lot of gray area. In fact it's mostly gray. Like my old man. Take away the beard, the drugs, the motorcycle, and the polygamy and you know what you've got? You've got *your* father."

"This is depressing," I said, walking over to check out Toy's bike.

"Oh well," Toy said, shrugging.

I was crouching beside the bike when I looked up. "So, I don't suppose you'll be settling anyplace nearby? I mean, like, so you could still kind of keep some of the old life intact?"

He walked past me and straddled the bike, nearly tipping me over. I stood and he looked straight down at his gas tank as he recited.

"My heart is warm with the friends I
  make,
And better friends I'll not be knowing;
Yet there isn't a train I wouldn't take,
No matter where it's going."

After a pause, I said, "Couldn't just say 'gotta fly' or something, huh, Toy?"

There was another pause, a strange one, full of stuff. Finally I came out with it. "Maybe I should go too," I said.

He answered immediately, as if he was prepared for it. "I don't think you'd like it where I'm going."

I looked all around. "Bet it's better than here."

Toy turned and fixed me with his under-the-hat stare. He threw his leg back over the bike and took the couple of steps toward me. He looked like now he was going to clock me, maybe for what I did to his mother. Good, I deserved it. I closed my eyes.

He kissed me. Barely touching my lips. Then so slightly, slipped me the tongue.

When I opened my eyes again he was there, all straightened up, hands on his hips, looking down on me. He had tipped his hat back on his head, exposing those eyes, those impossibly huge, unbelievably innocent brown eyes that he never showed and that didn't go along with anything else about him.

"So, still want to go there?" he asked.

I sat down on the curb, practically threw myself down, put my face in my hands. "That's not a place," I snapped angrily.

"What is it then, Mick? A color? A flavor? A race? An illness?" He sliced me with the tone.

I couldn't come up with an answer.

"Like I said, Mick, for you there are only black things, and white things."

I listened as the engine kicked over. By the time I looked up again he was gone.

The Difference

When I got back to the Sullivans' that
night, Mr. Sullivan was waiting for
me in the front room. He was sit-
ting in his wing-back easy chair, with his gun in
his lap.

"Mick," he called. "You had a visitor tonight."

"A big one?" I asked.

"Looked like a bear with a leather cap."

"I'm sorry, Mr. Sullivan," I said meekly.

"I ran him off. He went to your folks' place
first. Your old man directed him here."

I covered my eyes with my hands. "I'm sorry,
Mr. Sullivan," I said again.

"A fine guy, that father of yours."

"I know. You can shoot him if you want to."

"Ah, if only, boy. If only."

There, I thought, is a father. Sully's the luckiest guy of us all.

"I really am sorry, Mr. Sullivan. I appreciate everything you've done. I'm really, really sorry."

"I know you are, Mick," he said with a sigh. "It ain't even your fault. You can't help it. It just seems to follow you."

I started up the stairs when it seemed like he'd said what he wanted to. "It does, Mr. Sullivan," I said. "But I'm going to lose it."

"Hope so, Mick," he said.

I went right to the phone at the top of the stairs. I dialed Terry.

"Tomorrow morning," I said as soon as I heard his heavy, ignorant breathing. "You get Bobo and meet me. But it's not gonna be a show. No spectators, no Bloody Sundays, no Augie. Five A.M. at the O'Asis. There's room out back."

He listened quietly to it all. In the end he just hissed, "All right. It'll be great ta have ya back again, brother."

I couldn't sleep, couldn't even consider it. I had this thought over and over: I must have been the first person *ever* to tongue kiss both a guy and the guy's mother. Was there lower than me?

Maybe I should lay one on Carlo too when he catches up to me, so he doesn't feel left out.

A year ago I would have been out with Terry and Augie and Baba and Danny and the brave fat Cormacs all together beating Toy's ass.

I couldn't believe Mr. Sullivan was down there patrolling the lawn, harboring me instead of throwing me out there. Even though he probably half enjoyed it, he should have just cut me loose.

I had to do it for him. It was four in the morning when I went down, quietly packed my duffel bag, and shook Sully awake.

"I'm goin', Sul," I whispered.

He didn't open his eyes. "So go already," he said.

"No, I mean I'm really going this time. I'm not coming back after this morning. I'm going home."

He sat up, rubbing his eyes in the dark. "Really? You sure?"

"Ya," I said. "I'm taking care of everything this morning."

"I don't like the sound of that," he said. "You gonna be okay?"

"Ya," I said, though I had no idea. He was Sully, so he could see that.

"You want me to come with you?" he said, throwing his blankets off.

"Not necessary, Sul. But thanks."

"Thank god," he said, and pulled the covers up around him again.

I left him lying there, looking so comfortable. I stopped at the door and stared at him. "You have a good home, Sul."

"I know I do."

"I'm jealous of you."

"Line up with the rest of 'em, pal," he said through the muffling of covers.

Duran looked a little startled to see me so early. Then he started sniffing around and bumping me, looking for food. I hadn't even thought about that, but it could be risky trying to rely on just our friendship alone. But it was best to keep him empty and mean, and let him empty the old man's refrigerator when it was over.

It was kind of sweet, walking along with him in the just breaking daylight. There was a roll to his step that felt lively and strong. It was all new to both of us, walking this way to the bus stop, and with nobody else around yet, I wasn't even nervous.

The only rider on the bus was asleep, and the driver didn't even notice Duran, or else he just didn't let on. The dog fitted himself into one double seat and I took the one behind him. As he slobbered out the window just like any regular dog would, I scratched his ear and talked to him.

"You know, this really means a lot to me, what you're going to do here." He pulled his head in, looked at me, licked me with his sweaty brown tongue. "It won't take you long, and I don't think it'll be too hard for ya . . . and I won't ask ya to do it again, ever, I swear." He did it again, the licking thing.

We reached our stop and Duran was reluctant to get off. He loved the bus. "There'll be another ride later, c'mon," I said. And he came.

There was no Terry outside the O'Asis, and no Bobo. When I put my key in the deadbolt, I found it already open.

"How'd you get in here?" I said angrily as I pushed through the door. He sat with his feet up on a table.

"Jesus, don't ask me stupid questions," he sneered.

Then, as Duran ambled in behind me, the cockiness dropped from Terry's face. "Holy *shit*," he said, nearly tipping his chair over backward, catching himself on the table.

That felt good, and I held on to it for a bit,

folding my arms and leaning on Duran. "So where's Bobo?" I asked.

"He's out back already," Terry said, regaining his confidence quickly. "Bobo can't wait. I don't care how big your stupid spaniel dog is, Bobo's gonna eat his ass out. 'Cause Bobo's a *superior* animal."

Already, it wasn't fun anymore.

"Let's get on with it," I said.

"Fuckin' let's," Terry said.

Duran and I followed Terry to the back door. With a dramatic flourish, he flung it open. There in the middle of the lot, Bobo lay with his chin in the dirt. He raised his head ponderously, looked at us, but showed nothing like emotion.

I felt the rumbling of Duran's growl. I turned to see him rigid, the wiry, three-inch hairs standing straight up from the back slope of his skull almost all the way to his stumpy tail. All the teeth showed on one side of his mouth and he was locked into a pose like a giant pointer. He was leaning into me hard.

I looked back at Bobo, who slowly got to his feet. He looked at us, at Duran, and seemed to brace for something, but he didn't snarl, didn't get worked up. One ear looked about ready to fall off.

There it was. Everything. In one thirty-second mangling of that pathetic chump of a burned-out alcoholic dog, I was going to finally have it all. Terry was going to be gone. Gone for good. And I was going to get to watch him lick dirt all the way out. Finally, I was king. King of the game. King of *Terry's* game.

Finally I saw it.

King of the losers.

"Close the door!" I shouted.

"What?"

"Shut the door," I repeated. He did it. I started backing Duran away, across the bar, stroking and calming him. Terry followed us.

"What's your problem?" Terry spat.

"It's off. I'm out. He's out," I said.

"Bullshit," he screamed.

"Ya, well I'm doing it. Come on, Duran, I'm taking you home."

"You owe me a fight, boy," Terry said.

"Screw."

"Ya, well you still lose it all. You owe me the money, *and*"—he drew it out long, smiled, pointed at me—"annnnd, you're comin' home ta live. Wit me. I knew ya'd be back. You was never goin' nowhere."

I turned around, leaving Duran by the exit. I charged right up to Terry, stuck my finger in his face. "Screw," I said. "I'm goin' somewhere all right."

He snatched the hand I had in his face. He bent it back at the wrist, bringing me to my knees. "No, screw *you*," he said. Then he raised his other hand and slapped me. His slaps were harder than punches, with the whipping of his long bony fingers, and he slapped me again, and again, three times, four times. I could not get up off my knees as Terry slapped my face hard, pummeling the same side over and over.

"I should fuckin' kill you," he said. "Nobody'd fuckin' care." With those words he stopped slapping, held my arm straight up over my head, and kicked me high in the ribs with the toe of his work boot.

I fell, balling up under the table. The next thing I heard was the crashing of tables and chairs and scratching of claws. And Terry's full-lung scream.

I looked up and Duran was on him, pinning him to the floor with two massive paws on Terry's chest while biting, and yanking, on his arm.

"Duran," I said, scrambling over to them.

"Shut up," Terry screamed. The dog's fangs were sunk completely into one of Terry's biceps. He was clamped on it, squeezing. He looked like he was going to do it until he bit through. Which wouldn't take much longer.

"Fuck off, Mick," Terry screamed through his

screams. "I told you before, you don't never break up a dogfight." As he spoke, Terry kept trying to tug his arm out of the dog's grip, making it worse, making Duran dig further in. "I don't need you. Fuck off." Then he screamed, not at me or Duran, but into the air.

I listened to him, stood up, and stopped trying to stop Duran. The dog's eyes rolled backward, showing all white, as he twisted his head and the arm, making Terry scream and lamely punch at Duran's snout. Terry couldn't do anything with the dog, so he turned on me again.

"Fuck off, I told ya. I don't want you helpin' me. Don't do it. I wouldn't do it for you. I wouldn't ever do it for you, ya fuckin' loser."

That was it. It came through like a rocket burning away my fog. *It*. Finally. What I'd been looking for. I found it, and goddamn Terry was the one who gave it to me.

"You're right," I said. "You wouldn't ever do it for me. And *that's* the difference."

Against Terry's fading protests, I scrambled over to get Duran off him. "No," I said. "Duran, no. Stop. Stop now. Stop."

Duran growled, didn't look at me. "Stop it!" I said, slapping his back. "It's me." I angled down so that my face was looking right into his. Finally he turned his eyes up to me.

The flesh of his lip curled up, showing all of his long yellow teeth. For me this time. I'd actually thought, until then, that I had control of all this.

He looked at me for several seconds, considering me. Then he opened his great, wonderful, killer jaws, and let Terry's arm fall out. I jumped back. Duran looked coiled to leap on me until Terry rolled over, his mangled arm flopping after him like a string of raw sausages. When he caught Terry trying to wriggle spastically away, Duran slammed down on the back of my brother's neck. He toggled his head all around as he seized it. Like a dog does with a bone. Just like a dog does with a bone.

Terry stopped telling me not to help him. Terry stopped telling me anything.

As hard as I could, I punched Duran on top of the head. I punched him again. He paid me no mind, even though I heard the crack, felt the swelling between my knuckles already. I ran to the refrigerator and threw all the contents across the floor toward the dog. I opened the back door to let Bobo in, but Bobo had no intention of coming in. How many times had Bobo heard Terry say it?

The loser is *supposed* to lose.

Home

I was almost at Toy's house before I even realized where I was walking. My left hand was throbbing, so I shifted the duffel bag to my right.

By the time Toy came down with his knapsack slung over his shoulder, I was sitting on the bike, my bag in my lap, pretending to ride. Like a kid. I had my bad hand curled and tucked up into my armpit, like I was lame.

"What happened to you?" he said, pointing at the hand.

I looked at it closely, as if there was an answer there, then looked back to Toy. "I fell down, in the forest."

He nodded. "Ya," he said, "I believe I heard it."

"Is there still room on that train of yours?" I asked.

"Could be," he said.

"Well, I don't know if I'm going where you're going, but I figure we can ride together for a while."

Toy reached over to where his father's motorcycle was parked right next to his own, pulled a helmet out of the sidecar, and stuck it in my hands.

"I suppose we could, for a while."

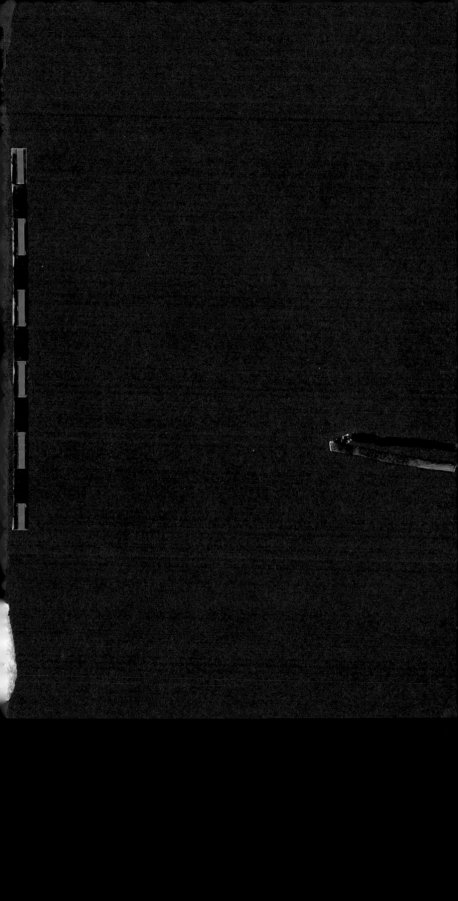